THE MIRROR OF GOOD CHARACTER

A four-year effort to take theory to practice

Lucy Frontera, Ph.D.
Executive Director, Ohio Partners in Character Education

Jennifer Jackson, M.A.
Literacy Coach and Character Education Consultant

The mirror of good character: A four-year effort to take theory to practice
by Lucy Frontera, Ph.D. and Jennifer Jackson, M.A.

Publisher: Character Development Group, Inc.
366 Bella Vista Dr., Boone, NC 28607
Toll-free: 888.262.0572
Email: Info@CharacterEducation.com
www.CharacterEducation.com

Library of Congress Control Number: 2012947244

ISBN: 1892056585

Printed in the United States of America

$19.95

ACKNOWLEDGEMENTS

This book is a compilation of strategies that were adapted or created by many people. The authors would like to thank Drs. Thomas Lickona and Matt Davidson for their outstanding work that provided the research upon which the project was based, as well as their ongoing advice and consultation. We would also like to thank Dr. Phil Vincent for his thoughtful and insightful comments on earlier drafts, and Dr. Cheryl Kish at the Ohio Department of Education for her support and encouragement throughout the project. We would also like to thank our tireless evaluators, Drs. Michael Corrigan and Doug Grove. And most importantly, we would like to thank our creative and enthusiastic character coaches Nancy Conaway, Katie Kreitzer, Mimi Khayo and Sherry Owens for their patience with us during the project and the hard work they put into making their schools a better place to work and learn. Special thanks to Sue Thuma, one of our teachers who although two years from retirement, completely embraced the project and changed the way she was teaching.

Our gratitude to our project steering committee for their dedication and valuable advice:

Roberta Camp Albert, The Ohio State University

Cliff Biggers, Race Relations Research, Inc/Newark Police Department

Stephanie Falor, Ohio Department of Education

Diana Leigh Morgan, Healthy Marriage Collaboration of Central Ohio

Monty Lobb, Ohio Center for Civic Character

Robin McAdams and Todd Wheeler, Nationwide Training Center

Kip Morse, Better Business Bureau of Central Ohio

Bonnie Nuxhall, Joe Nuxhall Character Education Fund

Mary Andres Russell, Character Council of Cincinnati
and Northern Kentucky

Tom Rutan, Ohio Department of Education

Jenny Smucker, Heartland Education Community, Inc.

Patti Spiegle, The Cortland Group, Inc.

Mike Thomson, It's All About Character

Lisa Weaver, Ohio PTA

Chip Weiant, BBB Center for Character Ethics

and the late Stephen M. Judah, author of *Essential Disciplines*

This project was supported by a Partnerships in Character Education grant from the US Department of Education and the Ohio Department of Education.

TABLE OF CONTENTS

PREFACE

This manual chronicles a four year (2006–2010) Federal Partnerships in Character Education Grant (CFDA 84.215) awarded to the state of Ohio. Ohio Partners in Character Education partnered with the Ohio Department of Education to implement the "Creating Smart & Good Schools" project, based on the work of Drs. Thomas Lickona and Matthew Davidson in the Smart & Good High Schools Report (2005).

Ohio Partners in Character Education is a program of the Better Business Bureau Center for Character Ethics, a 501c(3) organization devoted to promoting the highest standards of business ethics. The BBB's interest in character education stems from the needs of its member businesses for employees of good character. Surveys of what skills businesses want in new employees consistently include qualities such as the ability to work with others, being responsible, honest, punctual, cooperative, self-directed, having a good attitude and most importantly, having integrity. The Center supports character education to help the future workforce meet the challenge of ethical business practices and informed citizenship.

The project's primary focus was on developing student moral and performance character, and implementing strategies to improve school climate to help students make a successful transition to high school. Ten pairs of middle and high schools throughout Ohio participated in the study, all randomly selected from applicants to participate in the project. Five pairs were "implementation" schools and five were non-intervention schools. All participated in annual student, parent and staff surveys, and in addition, the implementation schools received staff professional development, material resources and a trained "character coach" to help provide on-site coaching in methods for integrating the model into the school, curriculum, and classrooms. Participants in intervention schools saw improvements and many changes were evident at the end of the project. We are pleased that the evaluation results confirmed our observations, and showed that the implementation schools had higher test scores, more positive attitudes, and a better school climate than the non-intervention schools. (See Appendix One, pages 125-133.)

The purpose of this publication is to share our "lessons learned" and the resources gathered or developed during the project. It is a "how-to" interspersed with concrete examples of strategies that worked. Although we focused on middle and high school, most strategies are equally applicable to elementary schools.

We hope you find this a valuable resource.

Lucy Frontera, Ph.D.
Project Director

Disclaimer

This book contains many resources that were developed by teachers; however it is likely that at some point in time they were based on other published materials. We have made every effort to identify and credit the original sources; however there are some materials that we were unable to identify an original source if in fact there was one. If we have inadvertently used other authors work without proper credit, we apologize in advance and ask for their forgiveness.

"If you wanna make the world a better place,
Take a look at yourself and then make a change.
I'm starting with the man in the mirror."

Michael Jackson,
"Man in the Mirror"

1

What Is Character Education and Why Do We Need It?

"Character education is a national movement encouraging schools to create environments that foster ethical, responsible and caring young people. It is the intentional, proactive effort by schools, districts and states to instill in their students important core, ethical values that we all share, such as caring, honesty, fairness, responsibility and respect for self and others."

The Character Education Partnership, a national advocate for character education

Two essential components of this definition are *intentional* and *core ethical values*. *Core values* because these are the values we can easily agree upon—qualities such as respect, responsibility, honesty, compassion, and fairness. These are the values that unite us and are crucial to a democratic society. *Intentional* because teaching and modeling good character must be intentional. By the nature of the roles they play, all educators serve as character educators whether their influence is positive or negative. It is when schools or individual teachers *intentionally* and *deliberately* integrate the development of character into the life of the school and classroom, that good character education happens.

Character education cannot be covered in ten minutes a day or viewed as a plug in once a week. It must be at the heart of the entire education program, embedded throughout. Character can't be taught in a course, it *is* a way of living. More specifically:

Character Education is not...	**Character Education is...**
a program or curriculum that can be purchased. Although there are many good materials or curricula for sale, purchasing them won't guarantee that students will develop good character.	an approach to education that focuses on positive relationships, a positive school climate, respectful community, engaging and challenging curriculum, and an ongoing pursuit to increase the moral excellence of our youth.
the sole responsibility of the counselor or a few teachers.	where everyone belongs and everyone has a voice. To be effective, character education must be infused in everything a school does. The goal of character education is for students and staff to "be their best selves and do their best work."
an attempt to teach religion or one group's values in the school.	a focus on *widely held, core, shared values* like respect, responsibility and caring. These are the values that we all agree upon and what unite us as a community, nation and world. The process of coming together and selecting the shared values of a school community is a crucial first step in any character education initiative.
an attempt to replace the parental role in teaching values.	a support to parents in their role as a child's first character educator. Schools that implement character education are not intending to take away the job of parents; rather they aim to target the traits and values that are needed to be good students, good workers and good citizens.
an add-on; it is not something else on a teacher's plate	what some in fact have said, "is the plate!"

Some teachers think that they don't have time or energy to add one more thing. They say they must focus on skills that will be tested and they don't have time for anything else. But, research shows that effective character education results in more time for learning, fewer discipline problems and a more positive school climate (see page 5).

The troubling facts for why we need character education

The need for developing character can be found anytime one turns on the television or reads the newspaper. From adults to teenagers to children, character is lacking in today's society. The economic crisis and political climate has brought a light to the issues surrounding the lack of character in the business world and lack of civility in government. The videotaping of teenagers beating up each other and posting it online has shed light on the issues related to the increasing violence among youth, exemplifying the lack of character schools are dealing with on a daily basis. The increase of bullying in schools and on the internet has resulted in documented cases of teen suicide. The statistics paint a frightening picture:

Teen violence

- Suicide is the second leading cause of death among 25- to 34-year-olds and the third leading cause of death among 15- to24-year-olds.
- Among 15- to 24-year-olds, suicide accounts for 12.0% of all deaths annually.
- In 2007, 14.5% of U.S. high school students reported that they had seriously considered attempting suicide in the past year and 6.9% of students reported that they had actually attempted suicide one or more times during the same period.(www.cdc.gov/violenceprevention/pdf/Suicide-DataSheet-a.pdf.1)
- 72% of eighth and ninth graders reportedly "date" and dating violence is a serious problem. Many teens do not report it because they are afraid to tell friends and family.
- One in four adolescents report verbal, physical, emotional, or sexual abuse from a dating partner each year.
- About 10% of students nationwide report being physically hurt by a boyfriend or girlfriend in the past 12 months. (www.cdc.gov/violenceprevention/pdf/TeenDatingViolence2009-a.pdf)
- Violent teen crime peaks at 3:00 p.m. (USDOE)

Bullying

- In 2007, nearly one out of three students in middle school and high school reported that they had been bullied at school during the school year. That means that 8.2 million students a year are suffering at the hands of bullies in school.
- One out of nine secondary school students, or 2.8 million students, said they have been pushed, shoved, tripped, or spit on during the last school year.
- Another 1.5 million students said they were threatened with harm, and 1 million students reported they had their property destroyed during the school year.
- In 2007, more than 900,000 secondary students reported being cyber-bullied. (Secretary of Education, Arne Duncan, remarks at Bullying Prevention Summit, August 11, 2010 www.ed.gov/news/speeches/myths-about-bullying-secretary-arne-duncans-remarks-bullying-prevention-summit)

"The famous broken windows theory suggests that the root problem in schools is not so much shootings on the playground but the message that disorder and disruption sends to the students—it's the broken window that goes unfixed that signals to students no one is really in control here and taking care of things. Just as good practice echoes through a school, so does bad practice."

Arne Duncan, August 2010

Disruptive classrooms

"Disruptive and disorderly schools are a serious problem because so little learning can take place in classrooms that are in a state of perpetual chaos." (Secretary of Education, Arne Duncan, Bullying Prevention Summit August 11, 2010)

- One in three teachers nationwide think that student misbehavior interferes with their teaching, and roughly the same proportion think tardiness and class cutting is impeding learning in their classrooms.
- In a recent national survey of 10,000 tenth graders in more than 650 high schools, three fourths of tenth graders said that other students often disrupted their classes.
- In urban schools 12% of secondary school teachers report that they were threatened with physical injury the previous year by a school student.
- 5% of urban teachers say they were actually attacked by a student the previous year. (Secretary of Education, Arne Duncan, Bullying Prevention Summit, August 11, 2010)

What does the research say about the effectiveness of character education?

Over the past two decades, schools and school districts throughout the United States, Canada and indeed throughout the world are giving character development a little more room at the table. Some have recognized that growing excellence in schools demands far more than a focus on curriculum. One's attitudes and inclinations such as integrity—choosing not to cheat, and perseverance—working to the best of one's abilities, do play a role in academic excellence. As a result nearly every state in the U.S. either has legislation or policies in place that mandate or strongly encourages character education to be a part of the curriculum and instructional practice.[1]

It makes sense to most that if our classrooms are filled with a higher percentage of students and teachers who show respect for others, practice responsibility, show resilience, trust their teachers and fellow students, practice kindness, and strive to develop moral and academic excellence, then we would most likely find our classrooms to be more conducive and vibrant environments for learning with far less distractions. For most students, increased academic achievement does not come from increasing one's IQ or mental aptitude but from giving them a vision for success and a reason to strive for excellence in all aspects of their work including achievement tests and assessments.

Does research support this view? Increasingly the answer is yes. The USDOE Partnerships in Character Education grant program (1996-2010) as well as other research studies have begun to provide a research base of knowledge that supports the use of comprehensive character education. Marvin Berkowitz, a leading researcher in the field, reviewed research on character education and related fields and concluded:

> **"Character education has been demonstrated to be associated with academic motivation and aspirations, academic achievement, prosocial behavior, bonding to school, prosocial and democratic values, conflict-resolution skills, moral-reasoning maturity, responsibility, respect, self-efficacy, self-control, self-esteem, social skills, and trust in and respect for teachers."[2]**

The Character Education Partnership recently published a white paper that summarizes research on character education, including data from its own National Schools of Character program. They conclude:

> **"Character education, when done effectively, can result in not only improved academic achievement, but positive youth development that leads to an increase in pro-social behavior and a**

decrease in risky behavior. The findings from all three studies are consistent, and a few key points stand out for effective programs:

- **Goals should be both explicit and ambitious.**
- **Professional development is critical.**
- **The whole school community should be involved, and everyone should have a voice.**
- **Adults need to be role models."[3]**

Handling resistance from stakeholders

The beginning of any project can be hindered by resistance for numerous reasons. Some are suspicious of a hidden agenda; some are tired of the "next big thing" of constant change prevalent in education and prefer to wait it out. Some are just set in their ways and don't want change of any kind. This section discusses some of the common issues that arise when starting a new school improvement initiative and how to avoid or handle them.

Be prepared

A reactive approach will be less effective than thinking about ways to be proactive. The key is to be prepared. When we are caught off guard by someone's objections to our ideas we tend to respond with frustration or defensiveness to save ourselves from embarrassment.

Use active listening

Actively listening means really listening to what the objector is truly saying. When teachers object or oppose an initiative or idea it may be because they interpret it as implying they are not effective at what they do. It is not easy to admit that your practice needs change, or your teaching methods and techniques are not effective in delivering instruction. Exercise patience and ask questions to get to the heart of the objection. The key is to acknowledge what the person has said and show appreciation for their input. There are some general strategies to handle hostile or resistant questions from staff, parents or board members:

- Remain silent for two or three seconds. This will allow time for you to process what has been said and hopefully prevent you from being defensive.
- Acknowledge what the person has said, such as "I can appreciate that...," "That's a natural reaction...," "I'm not surprised to hear you say that..."

- Ask direct questions in a calm manner, such as "That's interesting, but think about..."; "I can understand why you feel that way, however... (state the benefits of your point), "Yes, I used to feel that way, however...," "You're not alone in your feelings, however..."

Create opportunities for "open dialogue"

Lickona and Davidson (2005) refer to this as acknowledging the "elephants in the living room." Provide the opportunity for teachers and stakeholders to voice their feelings with their colleagues in a nonthreatening environment. This might also reveal underlying issues that need to be addressed. One way to accomplish this type of setting is to create small group or round table discussions. To stay on topic and to utilize time effectively, there must be some order and guidance before allowing this to take place. Use chart paper with 3-5 questions or statements to guide the discussions. Provide sticky notes for each idea to be noted. The group can then compile their answers and come up with a statement for each question on the chart.

What are some common objections to character education and how do I respond?

Whose values are you going to teach?

This is one of the first and most common reactions to the announcement that a school is going to start a character education program, and the easiest to address and calm fears. The answer is simply—"our shared ethical and prosocial values." This statement must be accompanied by a truly inclusive process to determine what the community's shared values are (see pages 25-30 for a discussion of how to go about this). When this type of objection is raised, most stakeholders are relieved and often become enthusiastic supporters when they learn the target is values such as respect and responsibility. This response also can address those who think character education is an attempt to teach religion or a particular political agenda in the schools.

That's the parents' job

Parents are the primary and most important moral educators of their children. Thus, public schools should develop character education programs in close partnership with parents and the community. Character education focuses on the core civic virtues and moral and performance values that are widely held in our society across religious and other differences. Under the First Amendment, public school teachers may neither inculcate nor denigrate religion. The values agreed to in the community may be taught in public schools if done so without religious indoctrination.

Also, most staff will acknowledge that, for a multitude of reasons, not all parents are able to model or encourage good character development. They know that some students do not learn this behavior at home, and that school and a caring staff may be a student's last and best hope to develop strong character.

I teach (math), not character

Many educators, particularly secondary teachers, have this reaction. They are uncomfortable with what they perceive as a non-subject matter teaching responsibility. This objection is most effectively addressed with a series of questions that you ask staff to respond to and record as a group on chart paper. Start with "What does it take to be successful in your class?" Most lists will include behaviors such as "students need to pay attention, show up for class on time, be responsible for their work, respect the teacher, fellow students and school property, and study hard." Then ask, "What kind of school do you want this to be?" Staff members usually say things like, "One where students and staff get along with each other, a caring atmosphere, mutual respect, hardworking, successful, etc." It is then a short leap to "That is what character education is all about—creating a safe, caring and supportive environment where students and staff are successful and can realize their highest potential."

They should know this by now, they should have learned it in elementary school

Obviously this is from secondary teachers, but at least they recognize schools play a role in character development! Elementary teachers, generally speaking, embraced the character education movement much earlier than middle and high schools, if in fact they ever abandoned it (see Thomas Lickona's *Educating for Character*[4] for an insightful discussion of the history of character education). Character development, learning how to get along in school and developing good work habits is part and parcel of the elementary curriculum, so there is little resistance of this type in elementary schools.

Secondary teachers, however, may voice this concern, and it is helpful to use the questioning strategy above as to what they think is needed to be successful in their classes. It is also important to remind them that developmentally, there are a whole new set of problems (sexting, cyberbullying, dating, drug use, etc.) that accompany adolescence, and students need help developing the character, skills and abilities to handle these challenges and be successful in school.

The Obedience School Fallacy

When I got my first dog, I took him to "Puppy Obedience School" where I naively thought they would teach him to be obedient. I soon found out that the only way for my puppy to learn to behave was for me to spend time teaching him. The puppy school instructor was there to give me techniques to teach my dog to sit, stay, stop—but I had to do the work. No one could "fix" my dog.

Schools often bring in character education speakers to talk to the students in hopes that they will change the behavior of the students—"fix them." While a good speaker will bring up the important vocabulary, provide inspirational stories to motivate the students, and create teaching opportunities for good character, they can't inoculate the students against poor character. One speaker compares developing character to bathing—you can't do that once or even yearly to be clean.

Character educator

Threats to implementation

Sometimes you will encounter little or no resistance, but staff buy-in may be low. There are two "dangerous" attitudes that often go along with this:

This is great—these kids really need this

The danger here is that you think these staff members are supportive, and they think they are too. But the underlying implication is that they expect someone to come in and "fix" the kids. They keep doing what they've always done. They think that they have good character and that they are modeling good character, which is not always true. Some staff automatically assume that character education requires students to change. However, one of the goals in implementing character education is to change the thought process of all staff to become more self-reflective and self-evaluative about their own behavior and methods. It is not all about "fixing" the students, but in greater fact, changing what is not working in the classroom and the school as a whole. This means that every teacher, staff member, and administrator must take a critical look at what is being taught, how it is being taught, and how responsive and receptive are the students? To keep doing what you have always done does not fix any situation, but to be willing to try new techniques and strategies to be more effective will be a step in the right direction.

We do a lot of this already

In an attempt to "sell" the project to the staff, one principal kept assuring the staff, "We already do a lot of this" so it wouldn't seem like he was asking staff to do one more thing. The problem was, staff interpreted this as not having to do anything. And that is what happened. This can also occur when we overemphasize integration—too much "integration" means intentionality gets lost. Character education isn't a separate subject, but it needs to be *deliberately* and *intentionally* included in the school culture, classroom procedures and instructional methods. Pointing out what the school already does is a starting point; however, *discussing effectiveness of existing practices and methods is crucial.* Ways to go about this and gain buy-in are discussed below.

Gaining staff buy-in and active support

There is no magic bullet for getting staff buy-in except a positive attitude and perseverance. In some cases the task is to get staff on board, in others it is a resistant or unenthusiastic administration. The following are strategies that worked for our project.

1. **Identify staff or colleagues who share a passion or willingness to participate.** Begin a study group or professional learning community. Share and celebrate successes with others. Eventually others will notice and want to join in. Early adopters will lead the way for others once it is evident that it does make a difference.

2. **Authentically include all stakeholders in planning.** No one wants to hear about a new "directive from upon high" that they are expected to implement without any chance for them to voice their concerns, fears or have a role in shaping. All stakeholders, including teachers, administrators, support staff, parents and students should have the opportunity to participate in the planning. That is why the touchstone or shared values exercise is so effective (see Chapter 3 for more detail).

Providing time for teachers to share their thoughts in a nonthreatening environment will be a step in the right direction to bringing more teachers to buy in to the initiative.

3. **Identify problem areas.** If you ask schools with effective character education programs how they got started, many will tell you that they had a problem with something—behavior, language, fights, absences, tardies—and they needed to find something to address it. A group of staff and parents studied the problem and offered character education as a solution. They implemented it gradually, adding new strategies as needed until it permeated everything the school did. So perhaps one can start with a discussion of what isn't working—in the school and in the classrooms. Use data to identify less visible problems (see page 31 for suggestions on assessments that can be used). Have a general discussion with the staff and provide them the opportunity to reflect on existing practices that might contribute to the problem. Invite them to voice their fears, concerns, and

ideas. By doing this, you are giving them the respect it will take to create a willing environment. Make sure to record their responses along with any ideas that are generated as well as positive and/or negative remarks.

4. **Create a "sell sheet."** Businesses often create a one page document with key information about their product or services that is used to sell. It needs to be concise and to the point, because everyone is busy and has limited time to attend to new material. One school created a "character education in a nutshell" document (see box on page 13) that explained what it was, why it was needed and how it would work. This helped orient staff. Giving too much information in the beginning is overwhelming. Finding a method to highlight the basics of the project will give just enough information to the staff so they will understand what character education is all about, making it less threatening. A similar piece can be developed for parents and community.

5. **Prove it.** Use data that shows how the methods and strategies used at other schools worked. Many will think, "What's in it for me?" Show the research (see above) that demonstrates that there is more time for learning and a more pleasant atmosphere in schools with character education. Visit other schools that have successfully implemented character education. A good place to start is to look for schools that have been named a state or national "School of Character." The Character Education Partnership maintains a list of these exemplary schools on their website (www.character.org/schools-of-character).

> "A major component of buy-in is leadership, and one thing all effective leaders have in common is the ability to influence with integrity."
>
> **Ivy Sea, Inc.**

6. **Be straightforward.** People want to know the whole truth. Be honest in your communication. No one believes anything is flawless—by acknowledging challenges upfront, you're more apt to gain the respect and trust that leads to active buy-in. Allowing staff to voice their hesitations, frustrations, and fears will allow you the opportunity for easement.

7. **"If you don't want to get on board—OK, but don't get in the way."** There was at least one person in each school that wanted no part of the project. The main thing was to not allow any one person to stand in the way of progress. Allowing them to have a voice is important, but as we know, people tend to feed off other's negativity. If you have a group of resistant teachers, try speaking with them individually, away from their supporters, to get their individual viewpoints. You may make more headway without their group of supporters. Being too pushy may

change a resistant teacher into a saboteur, which could be detrimental to any initiative. The point is to not allow a few resisters to stand in the way of development and improvement. If enough people are on board with any project, given time, the resistant teachers may eventually jump on board or they may even choose to leave the present environment.

8. **Constantly re-assess and evaluate.** Spending time regularly to celebrate success and address thoughts, concerns, or problems pertaining to the initiative is critical. If administration does not provide the time to address and revisit previous discussions then staff will assume it is not important enough and soon the initiative will lose momentum. This has to be ongoing but this is not to say that a great deal of time has to be given during meetings. Three to five minutes is adequate to touch upon the school's progress.

9. **Connect the initiative to an existing, well accepted initiative.** Our schools had the most success when they aligned the project to another school improvement initiative. They found ways to "supercharge" the existing program with the concepts and strategies of character education. In the next section we discuss how this was done with a number of common school improvement programs.

How does character education align with other school initiatives?

At the beginning of our project, one principal found himself with 6 different school initiatives, including our character education project, all competing for attention. To help coordinate, he created a graphic of six interlocking puzzle pieces with the goals of each initiative on a piece of the puzzle. He was trying in his own mind to see how they fit together so he could help his school be successful. Thinking of character education in this way is to see it as one more thing added on a full plate. When we met with him, we talked about how the character education project could be the "glue" that held the other pieces together, and it could in fact cement the entire school framework together.

Some projects also struggled when they started by trying to create a new set of structures—committees, vocabulary, events and projects. After struggling, they realized they needed to align with and amplify other established initiatives. Using language and structures that were already in existence helped with acceptance. But, it is critical to intentionally show how character education can amplify the current program. As discussed earlier, saying "we already do character education" implies that no change is needed, and staff members think they can keep on doing what they are doing now. Rather, take the approach that character education will "power up" existing efforts and make them more successful.

We discuss below two examples of strategies and resources for how character education can be aligned with PBS/PBIS and Asset Building.

Character Education in a Nutshell

What is character education?

Character education is a national movement creating schools that foster ethical, responsible, and caring young people by modeling and teaching good character through emphasis on universal values that we all share. It is the intentional, proactive effort by schools, districts, and states to instill in their students important core, ethical values such as caring, honesty, fairness, responsibility, and respect for self and others. Character education is not a "quick fix." It provides long-term solutions that address moral, ethical, and academic issues that are of growing concern about our society and the safety of our schools.

Why do we need character education?

As Dr. Thomas Lickona, author of Educating for Character, stated, "Moral education is not a new idea. It is, in fact, as old as education itself. Down through history, in countries all over the world, education has had two great goals: to help young people become smart and to help them become good." Good character is not formed automatically; it is developed over time through a sustained process of teaching, example, learning, and practice—it is developed through character education.

How does character education work?

To be effective, character education must include the entire school community and must be infused throughout the entire school curriculum and culture. Character education promotes core values in all phases of school life and includes proactive strategies and practices that help children not only understand core, ethical values, but to care about and act upon them. Caring teachers model and mentor, treat students with respect, set a good example, support prosocial behavior, and correct hurtful actions. The teacher creates a moral community that helps students respect and care about each other and feel valued within the group.

What is the goal of character education?

The goal is to develop students socially, ethically, and academically by infusing character development into every aspect of the school culture and curriculum. To help students develop good character, which includes knowing, caring about, and acting upon core ethical values such as respect, responsibility, honesty, fairness, and compassion.

Is character education as important as academics?

Absolutely. The social, ethical, and emotional development of young people is just as important as their academic development. Theodore Roosevelt stated: "To educate a man in mind and not in morals is to educate a menace to society." After all, we know that good workers, citizens, parents, and neighbors all have their roots in good character. Therefore, it is critical to create schools that simultaneously foster character development and promote learning.

Is religion a part of character education?

No. Parents are the primary and most important moral educators of their children. Therefore, public schools should develop character education programs in close partnership with parents and the community. Character education focuses on the core civic virtues and moral values that are widely held in our society.

PBS/PBIS *(Positive Behavior Supports/Positive Behavior Intervention Supports)*

One school had implemented PBS a few years earlier, so when they started their character education project, it was logical to align with it. They used character education to help them identify problem areas and define shared values. This led them to discuss in more detail what they wanted students to do. As they reflected on what was working and not working at the school, they became aware that many of the behavior issues were due to not having any specific and consistent expectations throughout the building. Up until that time, teachers had individual classroom expectations, which varied from classroom to classroom, but no explicit expectations for behavior outside the classroom. The resulting chaos in the hallways, cafeteria, and auditorium had led to a multitude of office referrals and the cancelation of assemblies and pep rallies. This realization led to the creation of explicit policies and a Behavior Matrix as part of their character education and PBS initiatives. They defined for each area of the school (hallways, lunchroom, assemblies, cafeteria, classroom, etc.) expected behaviors related to their shared values (respect and responsibility). The creation of this matrix unified the school, including staff and students. Teachers were expected to be present in the hallways and enforce a consistent set of rules. It gave all staff a common language when dealing with infractions. By defining behavioral expectations explicitly, everyone was on the same page, including students and staff. Excerpts from their policies and behavior matrix are included below. Bold italics show how they related this to their shared values. In addition, a template for teaching the school wide expectations to students is included.

4 PBS Elements

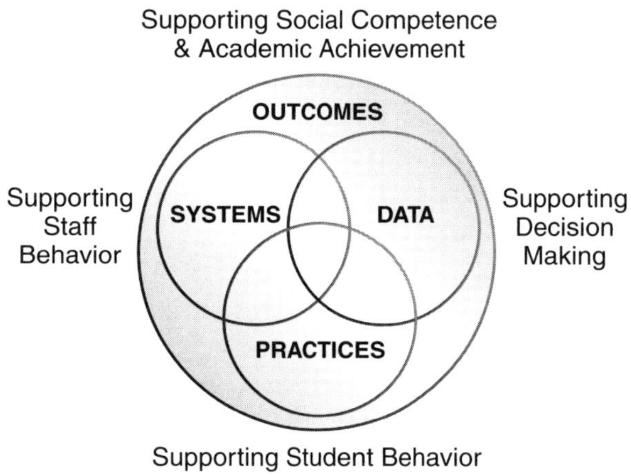

PBS Building Leadership Team

TARDY POLICY

Objective: *Recognizing that being prompt is an important skill to be successful;* *that being in class on time will increase the amount of time available for academic rigor;* that time for misbehaviors in the hallways is reduced when students are timely, it will be our policy that students will be in their assigned room *before* the bell rings.

Tardiness will be acknowledged with the following consequences:

- First Tardy—Verbal Warning
- Second Tardy—Standardized written note home signed and returned or phone contact
- Third Tardy—After School Detention and phone call home
- Fourth Tardy—Friday Detention
- Sixth Tardy—Office Referral

There will be a semester roll back for all classes.

The following routines will apply for teachers and staff:

- Bell attendance will be taken in Progress Book.
- Start class when bell rings; classes will be dismissed promptly.
- Hall passes from office/teachers will be used.
- No one leaves the room once they've entered.
- Students waiting to enter class should line up in a designated area.
- Teachers will monitor the halls at their doors when possible.

BEHAVIOR MATRIX		
	Respect	**Responsibility**
Hallways Stairs Walkways Sidewalks	• Speak in quiet voices • Keep hands, feet, and personal objects to self • Follow verbal directions immediately	• Carry all needed materials neatly and securely • Walk on the right hand side of the hall
Lockers	• Use only your assigned locker • Keep locker free from writing and other graffiti	• Keep your locker neat and organized • Know your combination and keep it private • Keep only your books, personal materials, and valuables stored in your assigned locker
Cafeteria	• Follow instructions of staff • Treat peers with respect	• Give help when is it needed • Keep your area clean • Follow cafeteria procedures
Restrooms	• Respect others privacy • Speak in quiet voices • Keep hands, feet and personal objects to self	• Wash your hands and throw away trash • Report problems to an adult • Exit immediately in proper dress code
Auditorium Gymnasium	• During a performance, be considerate by staying seated & listening to the performers • Remain quiet during serious or sad scenes • Show appreciation at the end of a performance by clapping	• Enter and exit in a safe and orderly manner • Stay with your class or group
Office- Student Waiting Center	• Wait quietly for your turn to speak with the secretary • Speak in a polite manner in a conversational volume • Follow directions of office staff or any adult staff member • If sent to the office for a disciplinary reason, discuss the details with the school administrator, not other students	• Get a pass from the teacher before reporting to the office, unless you are called to the office over the intercom • Upon arriving, inform a member of the office staff of the reason for your presence • Return to your class when your business in the office is completed
Bus circle	• Keep your hands, feet and personal objects to yourself • Follow verbal directions given by adults exactly and immediately	• Walk directly to your bus • Enter your bus and sit down quietly in your seat

Lesson Plan and Template for Teaching School-wide Behavioral Expectations
(**Bolded** words can be used as a template; *italics* are a specific example.)

Setting: *Hallways*

1. **Review the school-wide expectations and definitions for the setting.**
   - *Speak in quiet voices*
   - *Keep hands, feet, and personal objects to self*
   - *Follow verbal directions immediately*
   - *Walk on the right hand side of the hall*
   - *Carry all needed materials neatly and securely*

2. **Review the rationale for expectations.**
   - *In order for the school to be safe, orderly, and efficient, movement through the halls must be organized.*

3. **What do those expectations "mean" in this location?**

   a. **Positive examples (correct ways to behave—from matrix)**
   - *Student remains to the right side of the hallway*
   - *Students use a conversational volume in speaking with peers*
   - *Students help peers whose material have fallen to the floor*
   - *Students keep moving to class during transition times*

   b. **Negative examples**
   - *Student pushes another person while changing classes*
   - *Student yells to a friend at the end of the hall from him*
   - *Student shoves another student trying to use their locker*
   - *Student runs through the hall*
   - *Student hugs another student during the passing time*

4. **Provide an activity that allows practice for appropriate behaviors.**
   - *Create a video to illustrate the skill*
   - *Conduct a role play on the skill*

Asset building

Another district had extensive training in the Search Institute's Asset building (www.search-institute.org/) and understood the language, so they amplified that initiative with character-based programs that focused on student leadership to build student assets. Two of their initiatives were a Youth Leadership Team and a Character/Asset Treasure Hunt, described below.

Youth Leadership Team

The Youth Leadership Team focused on developing assets for students, teachers, and community. A group of students, identified by teachers as asset-deficient, received training in the 40 Developmental Assets. After training, the students held a professional development workshop for the high school teachers; two hours filled with hands-on activities, team-building fun, and an opportunity to thank their teachers for the difference they made in students' lives. This leadership team also shared the assets with local business people. They challenged them to take the assets into their homes and workplaces. Next, they held an "asset retreat" for 25 of their at-risk fellow classmates who needed that extra support at this time in their lives. Traveling by bus to a local church, they spent the entire day discovering their strengths and building upon them and building relationships with fellow classmates. One of the strongest results was that more than half of the at-risk group stepped up and volunteered to lead the middle school retreat, planned for the following month.

Character/Assets Treasure Hunt

One of the ways this school assessed evidence of asset building was with an activity in which the leaders had to make a list of observations throughout the school to prove asset building was making a difference. A few of their findings were: Smiling teachers, Principal's open door, quotes displayed, a student helping another student, a school touchstone, and a teacher greeting students at the classroom door.

The school also developed several tools to use with staff to develop relationships—see page 48 for examples.

Notes

1. For a list of state legislation and policies see http://www.character.org/uploads/PDFs/State_Character_Education_Legislation__2009-9-28.pdf
2. Marvin W. Berkowitz and Melinda C. Bier, (2004) Research-Based Character Education, *The ANNALS of the American Academy of Political and Social Science* 591(1), 72-85.
3. http://www.character.org/uploads/PDFs/White_Papers/White_Paper_What_is_it_How_does_it_work.pdf
4. Lickona, T. (1991). *Educating for character: How our schools can teach respect and responsibility.* New York:Bantam Books.

2

Our Model of Character Education

At the outset, we used the work of Drs. Thomas Lickona and Matthew Davidson in the *Smart & Good High Schools Report*[5] as the foundation for our project. The report is a rich resource of guidelines and best practices that were observed in the successful schools that Lickona and Davidson studied. However, it is not a "how to" manual and much of our journey was spent learning what could be replicated. As time went on, we added other elements to flesh out the original model. In this chapter, we describe the key principles and components that were most useful to our schools.

Key concepts from the Smart & Good model

Performance and moral character

Lickona and Davidson proposed a paradigm-shifting, re-conceptualization of character education in their 2005 report. They define character in terms of "performance character" and "moral character." Performance character includes the qualities needed to realize one's potential for excellence—such as diligence, perseverance, work ethic, positive attitude, and self-discipline. Performance character has a mastery orientation. Without performance character, students will not be successful even with the most rigorous curriculum. Moral character has a relational orientation and includes qualities such as integrity, justice, caring, and respect—ones that are needed for successful interpersonal relationships. "Moral character enables us to treat others and ourselves with respect and care, and

Performance Character has a mastery orientation. It consists of those qualities-such as effort, diligence, perseverance, a strong work ethic, a positive attitude, ingenuity, and self-discipline-needed to realize one's potential for excellence in academics, the workplace, or any area of endeavor.

Moral Character has a relational orientation. It consists of those qualities-such as integrity, justice, caring, and respect-needed for successful interpersonal relationships and ethical behavior.

ensures that we use ethical means to achieve our performance goals" (Lickona & Davidson, 2005, p.18). Whereas most character education prior to this had been focused on the relational aspects of moral character and thus readily embraced by elementary school educators, the newly targeted performance character traits were ones that particularly resonated with secondary teachers. They knew their students needed these traits to be successful in their classes, but they were so consumed with teaching content that they feared taking time to foster the development of performance character. Furthermore, many thought students should have learned all this earlier. Giving teachers strategies to develop performance character was extremely important to the project, although the most difficult to accomplish. It often required teachers to change the way they had been teaching for years, not an easy task. Much of the remainder of this book deals with the strategies that we implemented or that were developed by our schools to promote performance and moral character in their school and in their classrooms.

4 Keys[6]

The concept of the 4 Keys was extremely useful to the project—primarily because it was simple to implement and provided a helpful template for teachers to follow when planning their lessons. All staff received some form of professional development, formally or informally, that included how to incorporate the 4 Keys into their planning. Teachers were given examples of how they could follow these guidelines when planning lessons and assignments.

4 Keys to Developing Performance and Moral Character

1. **A community that supports and challenges** (expect excellence, provide a safe and supportive environment)
2. **Self-study** (students have regular opportunities to self-assess)
3. **Other study** (curriculum and extra-curricular activities include examples of high character and the path to excellence)
4. **Public performance** (regular, authentic opportunities to make school work public)

To reinforce the use of the 4 Keys, we featured 3 examples of its use at project schools in the project newsletter. We highlighted how staff members had used each of the keys in lessons or in the case of one principal, how they approached students at-risk of failure. (See http://www.charactereducationohio.org/programs/creating-smart-and-good-schools-project/newsletter-archive/)

Alignment audit[7]

As discussed by Lickona and Davidson, the major purpose of an alignment audit is to align all school (and classroom) practices with the desired outcomes, in this case ethics and excellence. Everything the school does should contribute in some way to helping students develop performance and moral character, which will help them become successful.

The alignment audit was particularly helpful for each school to identify where change was needed most. By reviewing school policies, practices and procedures, they were able to identify those that weren't working or where new ones were needed to solve problems. Oftentimes, schools initiate procedures to respond to particular needs or problems, but don't review them once the problems go away or are no longer an issue. For example, one school had previously eliminated all extra-curricular activities (dances, student council, etc.) because of discipline problems in the past. Although they were still working on discipline problems, they decided that they needed some of these extra-curricular activities to help students develop the performance and moral character skills that would help the school solve their discipline problems.

The alignment audit is also designed to identify which school or classroom practices do not contribute to developing excellence or ethics. Most schools found that each teacher had their own set of rules and expectations for the classroom, which when wildly different across classrooms, is confusing to students. In one middle school, this led to a year-long effort to create common discipline guidelines for each grade level, with increasing expec-

Auto mechanics align the wheels so the vehicle is pointed in a straight line. Curriculum alignment follows the same principle, with the "wheels" being curriculum, instruction, standards and assessment. Research indicates this kind of alignment can point a school or district toward improved student achievement.

But there's a catch: It can't be done in 30 minutes or less—it's more a process than an event. And, all the work can't be done in one "shop" (different components are done at the state, district and school levels).

tations for responsibility and behavior at each grade level. Other schools worked on aligning expectations and policies within departments so that there was more consistency between classrooms of the same subject.

School transitions

A primary focus of the project was to have students develop the performance and moral character skills needed to make successful transitions to high school and beyond. Data shows that the largest number of students drop out within the ninth and tenth grade years, due to the failure of students to successfully complete high school coursework, become engaged in the life of the school, or find meaningful and relevant learning experiences.[8] Each of the implementation schools enhanced or developed practices and programs to help eighth grade students make a successful transition to high school. Several schools instituted freshman only days, some created freshman advisories, and one went so far as to develop a "Freshman Academy" to provide academic and social support for struggling freshmen. There is more information about transition strategies in Chapter 11.

Secondary literacy strategies

The project also included, as a supplementary strategy, the use of content area reading skill development to help students develop performance character. Research has identified comprehension of complex text to be an essential component of secondary reading instruction and a major predictor of success in postsecondary education and the workplace.[9,10] Sadly, according to statistics gathered on the ACT, only about half of high school students have developed the reading skills necessary to succeed in college,[9] and few secondary teachers teach reading skills at all.[11,12] Further, poor reading skills often prevent students from mastering other subjects,[13] and experts recommend reading skill development in all subjects, not just English and Social Studies.[14] Integrating the development of performance character with the development of secondary literacy skills provided students and teachers with tools for success. A number of the strategies used are included in Chapter 8.

"Character coaches"

Our project also utilized "character coaches" at each of the five implementation districts. The coaches were charged with providing professional development to staff on the key concepts of the model, garnering staff support and developing in-house leadership, and providing individual coaching to staff on how to integrate performance and moral character in the classroom.

Coaches have become more common in schools over the past decade—primarily as a way to provide professional develop and retain teachers. Literacy coaches are the most prevalent—followed by math and instructional coaches. "Character" coaches are a new concept, so our coaches had to be creative and independent because there was no model or training manual to follow. They were charged with "rejuvenating" staff to be their best self and do their best work also. This model enhances and develops support for each teacher's needs.

According to the National Commission on Teaching and America's Future (2008), one-third of all new teachers leave after three years. In some school districts half of the new hires are replaced every five years. The Commission also found that 46 percent of new teachers are gone within five years.

Not all districts or schools can afford curriculum coaches, let alone one charged with developing character. However all of our schools said they would keep the coach on staff if they had funds after the project was over. Evidence is mounting on the positive impact coaches can have on teacher quality. For example, Atul Gawandi reports that "six months after a workshop, less than 20 percent of educators actually use the skills learned."[15] In contrast, he says, 85 percent of educators who have been coached are still using those skills six months later. We believe this is one of the most important "take aways" from our project, the value that coaching can have on school climate and teacher quality. In Chapter 6 we outline strategies for staff development that schools can to utilize to imitate having a character coach, and in the remaining chapters we present our "lessons learned" from the project. It is a "how-to" interspersed with concrete examples of strategies that worked.

Notes

5. Lickona, T., & Davidson, M. (2005). *Smart & good high schools: Integrating excellence and ethics for success in school, work and beyond.* Cortland, NY: Center for the 4th & 5th Rs. Washington, DC: Character Education Partnership.
6. Lickona & Davidson, 2005, p. 29
7. Lickona & Davidson, 2005, p. 69
8. Bridgeland, M., DiIulio, J., & Morison, K. (2006). *The Silent Epidemic. Perspectives of High School Dropouts.* A report by Civic Enterprises by Peter D. Hart Research Associates for the Bill and Melissa Gates Foundation.
9. ACT, Inc. (2006). *Reading between the lines. What The ACT Reveals About College Readiness in Reading.* Iowa City, IA.
10. American Diploma Project. (2004). *Ready or not: Creating a high school diploma that counts.* Washington, D.C.: Achieve, Inc.
11. Ericson, B.O. (2001). Reading in high school English classes: An overview. In B.O. Ericson (Ed.), *Teaching reading in high school English classes* (pp1-22). Urbana, Il: National Council of Teachers of English.
12. Meltzer, J. (2002). *Adolescent literacy resources: Linking research and practice.* South Hampton, NH: Center for Resource Management.
13. Joftus, S. (2002). *Every child a graduate.* Washington, DC: Alliance for Excellent Education.
14. Kamil, M. (2003). *Adolescents and Literacy: Reading for the 21st Century.* Washington, DC: Alliance for Excellent Education.
15. Varlas, L. (2012). What Makes Good Teachers Great. ASCD Conference Daily, April 18, 2012.

3

Getting Started

School touchstones

Each school began the project by creating a school touchstone. The process of creating a touchstone helped bring the school community together, helped them create a set of shared values and fostered conversations about what their mission was and what they wanted for their students. A touchstone should not be used as a set of commandments. Ideally, the touchstone becomes a guide for thinking and acting for students and adults in the school community.

Many schools already have mission statements or "mottos"—but a mission statement or motto is simply not enough in most cases. A touchstone defines shared values, promotes a sense of belonging, and, hopefully, a sense of pride. It is the foundation upon which all other school activities,

Definition of a Touchstone

A school touchstone is a written statement describing the identity, or culture, of a school by identifying its core values. Ultimately, the touchstone says, "This is who we are and who we're striving to be."

Purpose of a Touchstone

A touchstone promotes a sense of belonging, unity and pride. It is the foundation upon which school activities, lessons, and procedures can be based. A touchstone states very clearly the expectations for the entire school community.

lessons, and procedures can be based. The touchstone provides a sense of unity. It states very clearly the expectations for the entire school community. When values are met, people tend to feel a sense of satisfaction, harmony, or rapport.

Each school had a different approach and created a different product. Several are described below.

1. Student-centered approach

The only way to truly garner ownership is with student input.

This school started with student input by having each class conduct the activity described below:

- Discuss the definition of a touchstone, as well as its purpose.
- Define what makes a person "smart." Record these traits on chart paper.
- Define what makes a person "good." Record these on chart paper.
- Review the lists. Ask the students how many of them would like to attend a school where all of its members (students, staff and volunteers) reflected those traits. As expected, almost all students raised their hands. Ask students that if most (or all) students would like to be a part of such a school, then didn't those traits reflect the values we should hold? Give each student two stickers. The students mark which word or phrase listed under each heading ("Smart" and "Good") was the "key" to that heading.
- In the end, the students had a visual of what that particular class felt was key to being smart and good. Even though each class had a slightly different list of traits, there were still obvious common threads.

Once each class completed the activity, the following steps were taken:

> **Canton South High School**
> **Wildcat Pride**
>
> We consistently demonstrate respect.
>
> We are responsible for what we do.
>
> We consider our actions
> and choose to excel.
>
> **This is our legacy!**

- Homeroom leaders met as grade levels to analyze the input. They first noticed that five common values stood out: common sense, education, effort, respect, and positive attitude.
- Homeroom leaders then met as a whole. They reviewed the common values and created action statements for them, so that they knew what each value "looked like." During the televised morning announcements, they displayed the draft, so that homeroom leaders and the teachers could receive suggestions from all of the students.

- Because the goal was to create something the whole school community could remember, the next homeroom leader meeting focused on paring down the first draft. They began with the suggestions from the homerooms. After making a few modifications, they decided to focus on just the action statements of the touchstone, which allowed them to reduce the wording. They again took this back to the student body for feedback.
- At the next meeting, they pared down the five action statements to three and gave the final draft to the homeroom leaders and presented it over the announcements.
- They created small posters, allowing the touchstone to be a part of every classroom, hallway, and office.
- The homeroom leaders then focused on activities to encourage students to learn and pay attention to the touchstone. The teachers were also encouraged to utilize the touchstone in their classroom in any way and at any time.

2. Student-staff input

Another example for creating a touchstone is having both students and teachers participate in the creation process as described below:

A touchstone can guide thinking and acting.

- Teachers and administrators discuss during a staff meeting what they would like to see in and from students. Talk about school pride, spirit, and positive tradition.
- Place chart paper outside classrooms with two columns labeled, "Things to preserve and celebrate," and "Things to improve," and have students and teachers write in their suggestions.
- Staff and student leadership team collects the sheets and looks for patterns. Combine this information with suggestions from the staff meeting. When the patterns have been identified, begin creating phrases or sentences to be considered for the touchstone such as, "We stand up for each other."
- Record the phrases or sentences on chart paper(s). Place these chart papers where all students will be able to give input, such as the cafeteria. Simple instructions suggesting that each student put a check by the phrase or sentence they like best will allow for student input. Allow ample time for students to actually be given the opportunity to mark their choice.
- After the majority of students have marked their choice with a dot or check mark the charts may be taken down. The team of students can now craft a draft of the touchstone based on the results of the charts they collected. The phrases or sentences with the most checks will be the ones used in the touchstone.

- Distribute a draft of the touchstone to parents, students, staff, and community members for feedback.
- Have leadership team of students and staff make final "tweaks" to the touchstone based on community feedback.
- Once the touchstone is finalized, post it ubiquitously. Consider printing it on every school newsletter, on magnets, bumper stickers, on school t-shirts, on the back of school ID cards, and on posters throughout the school.

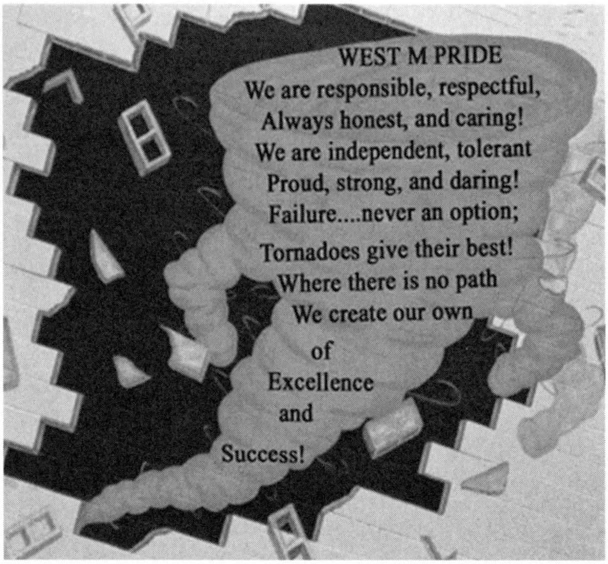

3. Competition

One school created their touchstone through a school wide (junior and senior high) competition. The English teachers gave a definition of what character traits their school mascot had and why one of their well-known coaches had chosen it as their mascot (a husky dog). Students could write an acronym, phrase, or logo picture. They had the freedom to do whatever they wanted for describing the "Husky Way." The teachers then helped to pick the five top choices, and the whole student body voted on them. Leadership staff then combined a couple of the ideas from other entries, along with teacher's ideas until they found an overall logo/phrase that described their mission using the mascot.

If you make an intentional effort to utilize student input and imbed the touchstone in everything you do as a school, then the students, staff, parents, and others will use it as a reference. Keep in mind that students from all levels of ability should be considered to be a part of the touchstone process. As you define the student leadership selection process, think about the students who would benefit from being chosen, but also show potential in leadership. Try to avoid choosing only the oft-chosen popular students. This is an opportunity to bring together students with various skills.

The following **do's and don'ts** will help keep a focus on the desired outcome of a school touchstone:

- **Do** use words and phrases that are easily understood by all.
- **Don't** use "big" words just for show.
- **Do** make the touchstone part of everything you do in and out of the classroom.
- **Don't** just create posters to be hung on a wall for decoration.
- **Do** use the touchstone for all to use as a guide for reflection.
- **Don't** forget that all stakeholders are a part of the touchstone.
- **Do** use the touchstone as a learning tool.
- **Don't** lose sight of the purpose of the touchstone.

Students want to know their school's beliefs and boundaries because they want to understand the implications of their choices and decisions.

One of the schools noted that the success of their touchstone was because it was created by staff *and* students and that it was read daily to introduce announcements. Students even created touchstone videos to define and give examples of touchstone-worthy behavior. The meaning of their touchstone also shines through by illustrations created by students that depict the meaning and purpose of their school.

Additional resources for developing a Touchstone

- www2.cortland.edu/centers/character/newsletters.dot Spring 2009
- **Millbrook High School** www.millbrookcsd.org/highschool/principal.html
- **The Integrity Team—Richmond Rose** http://teacherweb.com/ON/RichmondRosePublicSchool/Integrity/ap2.stm (Click on "Touchstone video.")
- www.theattribute.ca/articles/touchstone.pdf (newsletter devoted to developing a touchstone)
- **Upper Blue Elementary School** (Summit School District) summit.k12.co.us/schools/UBE2001/principal.html Also look at the September 06 newsletter.
- **Hamilton Central School** (This one had a neat celebration.) http://hcs.colgate.edu/district/pubs/ The March 07 newsletter has the touchstone in it.
- **Carson Elementary School** (Denver) http://editweb.dpsk12.org/carson/principal
- **Denver Public Schools Manual** www.dpsk12.org/manila/programs/charactereducation/EdforCharinDPS.pdf This is a GREAT resource. Pages 37-44 have a "how-to" for touchstones.
- **Massapequa High School** (See page 2 of document.) www.msd.k12.ny.us/files/filesystem/MHS%20Student%20Handbook%202006%20-%202007.pdf

Identifying and assessing problem areas

Each project school employed some method to assess their problem areas and to gather data on the perceptions of students, staff, and parents. Most schools regularly collect data that can be used at the outset—tardies, absences, discipline referrals, grades, etc. All of these—including trends up or down will point you in the direction of many of your problems. Some schools had implemented sophisticated computerized tracking systems that provided a wealth of information about where and when discipline problems were taking place. Another school used data on grades, discipline and absences to identify students who were experiencing problems and needed additional services.

In addition to the use of school data, there were two basic approaches to assess the problem areas—issues that might not show up in school data. These approaches were to employ attitudinal surveys or to create a staff committee. Many combined the assessment process with the development of the touchstone, so they not only collected information on what problems were present, but what the stakeholders wanted to see. Each approach is described below, with tools and resources.

Surveys

There are numerous school climate surveys available for schools, some of which are "open source" (free), others are proprietary and involve a cost. All of our projects used open source surveys, or developed their own.

When using a survey, it is important to select an instrument (or questions) appropriate for the audience, that get at the issues you want to gain perspective on (such as bullying), and most importantly, that will be easy to compile results for. One of our project schools used an excellent survey and distributed it widely to staff and parents, but had underestimated how difficult it would be to compile the results of a paper and pencil survey for several hundred respondents! If you wish to do a formal survey, but have limited funds for compiling results, we recommend

Open source resources for assessments

- 11 Principles (www.character.org)
- School as a Caring Community Profile-II (www2.cortland.edu/centers/character/assessment-instruments.dot)
- CREE—Collective Responsibility for Excellence and Ethics (www.excellenceandethics.com/assess/cree.php)
- The book *Evaluating Character Development* by Ed DeRoche (available at www.charactereducation.com) is an excellent source of surveys and resources for assessment.

using a service such as "surveymonkey.com" or asking your IT or technology department to help you set up a computerized survey.

The formal, independent evaluation of the project led to the development of a very comprehensive set of surveys for students, parents and staff which are now available commercially. For more information about this assessment system, see http://www.mdedinc.com/

Committees

Most of our schools created school committees to assess problem areas in their schools, and most collected information from other staff as to their perceptions. The following are tools that can be used by committees or by the entire staff in staff meetings to identify and develop plans of action.

1. Problem Statement: A problem statement is a concise description of the issues that need to be addressed by a problem solving team and should be presented to them or created by them before they try to solve the problem. The primary purpose is to focus the attention of the team. The guide below is an effective template for using a problem statement. Large chart paper works well to organize answers.

PROBLEM STATEMENT

Identify the following situations.

1. **CURRENT SITUATION:** What is the problem?
2. **DESIRED SITUATION:** What would you like to see?
3. **HOW DO WE GET THERE?:** Ideas to obtain the desired situation.

2. Simple Survey: One group asked staff to respond to the question "What are the top three areas of concern you have for our school?" This concern can be for any area of the school (classroom, staff, community, etc.). Once concerns are written, they can be organized by likenesses or affinity. This method allows participants to view the concerns of others in a nonthreatening way. It also provides validation to see that others may have the same concerns as you. Once the concerns are compiled, the next step is to generate ideas to resolve the concerns. This data gathering was easy to compile and provided sufficient evidence to begin planning and addressing areas of concern.

3. Issue Bin: An issue bin is a great way to get the staff communicating and thinking about their concerns by narrowing the focus of the questions. For each focal question use a piece of chart paper, label the question, statement, or phrase at the top. Teachers and staff can now work their way from one chart to the other writing their concerns or thoughts for each. One way to do this is to place chart paper on the walls in an area where teachers will be allowed the freedom to revisit and add to as necessary, for example, the teacher's lounge. This technique was used at one of the schools and had many responses to the issues. When questioned about the process, many teachers stated how nonthreatening this method was because you were not forced to speak your concerns out loud.

CAUTION: One downfall to this strategy was that the issues were never revisited; so many teachers then felt it was pointless when there was no follow-up. In order for this strategy to be successful, the administrator must follow up with the responses to the issues.

4. Issue reflection: Another effective way of getting staff to communicate their concerns and allow them the opportunity to voice their ideas is to have them write their issue on a piece of paper. Circulate the papers, or post on the wall of the teacher's lounge and ask everyone to reflect or comment on those concerns that they share or have addressed or solved in some way. Give staff a time limit to respond. At the end, each teacher will have several responses to their original concern. Many teachers have responded that this technique gives them practical ideas as well as validation that they are not alone with their concerns. Concerns that are shared by many that don't have good solutions may create the basis for action.

4

School Leadership: The Role of Administrators

Need for principal support and leadership

Many teachers we have talked with over the years have said they would love to have character education at their school, but their principal cares only about test scores. We have spent a lot of time trying to convince principals that character education leads to better test scores! Fortunately, research is mounting that character education does lead to higher test scores—as well as a more positive school climate and more positive attitudes of students and staff.

> "If your actions inspire others to dream more, learn more, do more and become more, you are a leader."
>
> **John Quincy Adams**

That said, the role of principals, as well as other administrators and superintendents is not only to support character education, but to *model* it and *lead* it. Just as a CEO or company president sets the tone for a business, the principal's actions and behavior—overt or covert—creates the school climate. Character education expert Dr. Marvin Berkowitz believes so fervently in the power of principals, that he developed the "Leadership Academy for Character Education,"[16] a year-long learning experience for administrators that includes study, self-reflection, strategic planning and coaching.

Without the support of an effective leader, school policies, procedures, and school climate will fall short of its true potential. When a school lacks effective leadership, minimal learning takes place. School leaders must provide strong leadership that sets a tone for the daily operations of the school community. In the absence of such leadership, discipline breaks down, academics falter, and a sense of organized chaos reigns. School leadership is not just about walking the halls and telling students to "tuck in their shirts." Rather, it is about dynamic modeling that encourages collegiality and promotes excellence in every aspect of the school community. Good leaders are respected by the entire educational community.

So how should a principal desiring to lead with character begin? Simply stating to the staff that they are going to partake in character education will not get too far. The principal must create an atmosphere where teachers and staff can effectively come together in a productive setting. Our project schools utilized a number of strategies and tools that principals and administrators can use to create a positive school climate that promotes respect and learning by all.

Strategies and tools for principals

Creating a supportive environment

Time is a major factor in the life of a school. There is the need for classroom time, time for planning, and time for staff meetings, etc. How principals allocate time reflects their priorities and tells staff what is valued. Just as with curriculum, to support character education and positive school climate, sufficient time must be devoted to it. It is the responsibility of the principal or administration to ensure sufficient time for planning purposes, such as working common planning time into the schedule so staff can coordinate curriculum, share best practices and build collegial relationships among staff. For students, adding time for advisories or homerooms to foster positive relationships can "pay dividends" with fewer discipline problems that take away time for learning.

How Can Principals Use the 4 Keys?

1. **A community that supports and challenges:** encourage students *and* staff to set high goals for performance each year.
2. **Self-study:** encourage staff to reflect on their progress as educators using effort rubrics and other measures.
3. **Other Study:** provide opportunities for staff development and for visiting exemplary schools.
4. **Public Performance:** Encourage service learning and schedule regular opportunities for students to display their work to parents and the community.

Common planning time

One of the project schools had common planning time built in before school each day. On certain days the time was devoted to departmental planning to align curriculum, and other days to grade-level planning. Occasionally this time could also be used to share new practices or provide in-service in character education. Adding time to the school day for planning is most often a contractual issue, and therefore not always under the control of the principal. In those cases, scheduling staff time within the school day so that grade-level or department staff share free periods for planning is the next best option.

Ensuring consistent policies

Another common issue among schools was inconsistent policies. These issues often centered on grading and discipline policies. Many schools found that their grading policies did not reflect their emphasis on developing performance and moral character, nor their desire to create a positive school climate. Discipline policies were also reviewed and many schools made changes to align them with their touchstones. Because of their importance, these issues are addressed in separate chapters (see Chapters 7 and 10).

Active leadership

The most effective principals assumed an active role in the project. They did not necessarily serve on the leadership committee, but they encouraged staff to participate, provided time for meetings and projects, listened to and supported what staff wanted to do, and used the shared common language of the touchstone with students and staff. The following are strategies employed directly by some of these effective school leaders:

A leader is one who knows the way, goes the way, and shows the way.

- **Morning announcements.** One principal personally delivered inspirational quotes each day with the announcements and encouraged and challenged the staff and students to discuss those quotes throughout the day. He noted that students would come up to him in the hallways to discuss a quote, and that one day when he was out of the building and couldn't deliver the announcements, several students asked him where he was! They were listening.
- **Visibility.** Actively involved principals made sure everyone saw them throughout the building. They visited classrooms, PE classes, tech classes, etc. They were a part of the class and joined in when appropriate. Greeting students at the door is not just for the elementary school principals; it speaks volumes throughout the middle and high school as well.

It tells the students (and staff) that you know who they are and care about them. Dedicate as much time as possible to greet students upon entrance to the building and be visible in the hallways between classes.

- **Instructional leadership.** Effective principals encouraged staff to share effective pedagogy with others. They provided positive feedback after observations of teachers and when needed, offered suggestions on ways to improve their instruction. Recognizing that there is not enough time to offer the support some teachers need, they developed a way to pair or team teachers together to share techniques and strategies. They encouraged them to strengthen and build relationships with each other to create a support network and work to break down the "silos" that often occur in schools. Team building techniques and developing support networks are vital to insure that staff feel a connection with each other.

Leadership is a process by which a person influences others to accomplish an objective and directs the organization in a way that makes it more cohesive and coherent.

- **Openness to staff input.** Effective principals had systems in place for staff to bring up concerns. Although they couldn't solve every problem or make all staff happy, staff felt that the principal would listen and take a concern seriously.
- **Follow-up.** Often principals acknowledge a problem exists, and perhaps a solution is suggested, but there is no follow-up. Principals who organized the support teams and consistently checked on the progress had better outcomes.
- **Team orientation.** Exemplary principals provided guidance and feedback to their faculty and staff and created a team-oriented climate in the building. They encouraged and provided time for team building activities for staff.

Communication

Some of the most common problems we saw were decisions being made by administration or central office that affected staff but did not involve, nor were communicated, to staff. At the beginning of the project, one teacher told us that she learned about the hiring of a new principal at the high school from the newspaper! To garner buy-in and ownership for any initiative, staff and students must have a voice in making the rules and setting expectations (see Chapters 8 and 9 for how this can be accomplished in the classroom). Even when decisions must be made by administrators, it is essential that all staff and students are well informed of any decisions.

Checklist for Principals

- Do I reflect on my own behavior regularly and honestly?
- Do I purposely try to exhibit integrity, honesty and respect throughout the day?
- Am I approachable and friendly to staff, students and parents?
- Do I support the staff and listen to their concerns?
- Do I encourage personal responsibility?
- Do I stay current on educational research and trends and am I able to educate and prepare others?
- Do I give clear expectations for staff and students and hold all accountable?
- Am I cautious not to play favorites?
- Do I regularly include stakeholders in the decision-making process?
- Do I spend time in staff meetings discussing the importance of character and encouraging staff to self-reflect?
- Do I acknowledge and celebrate accomplishments of my staff?

Be the message

Principals who modeled what they expected from their staff got more desirable outcomes and gained the cooperation of their staff. When the principal does not allot time to an initiative or hold staff accountable for it, the faculty quickly learns that it is not important. The checklist above was derived from what one staff said they wanted from a principal. It can be used as a self-reflection tool for principals.

Setting expectations for staff and students

One of the 4 Keys is "a community that supports and challenges." Effective principals set clear expectations for staff and students, and provide support needed for them to meet expectations. For example, one principal asked the ninth grade math teachers to send her the names of all students who were failing Algebra at the end of the first quarter. She called the students into her office, but rather than admonish them and warn them to work harder, she asked them about how they liked high school and what problems they were having. Once the students understood that the purpose of the meeting was to understand their problems and point of view, they began to relax and speak openly and honestly. They talked

> "The task of the leader is to get his people from where they are to where they have not been."
>
> **Henry Kissinger**

about the programs that were helpful and concerns they had with homework and class expectations. The principal also told them about how she had struggled with math in high school, but because she knew how important it was for graduating and going on to college, she persevered. They talked about what kind of help they would need to be successful in Algebra, and the principal found a volunteer tutor to come in a few days a week to help these students improve in math. The result? The students' grades improved. The principal had demonstrated to these students that she cared about them, but also that she expected them to be successful and she found the support they needed to be successful.

Another principal set the expectation for staff that they make six calls to parents each month—and that at least half of them be positive. He held the staff accountable by requiring that they turn in phone logs of their calls.

Communicating expectations for the school year at the beginning of the year and following through with those expectations throughout the year is a way to prove your high quality leadership skills.

Hiring for character and new staff orientation

There is a saying in business that you should be "slow to hire but quick to fire." Unfortunately, few businesses, or schools, practice that advice; in fact it is usually the opposite. Although the "quick to fire" metaphor doesn't normally apply to schools, the advice "slow to hire" is relevant. What is meant is that the process of hiring a new employee should be a deliberate and careful consideration of the person's character, skills and fit with the organization. In business, most terminations are due to character rather than lack of job skills. For schools, the authors have observed over time that teachers or principals rarely lose their jobs, but when they do it is usually for serious moral lapses, such as inappropriate relationships with students, inappropriate disciplinary actions or financial missteps. Identifying these types of employees prior to hiring may be difficult, but a principal and district that makes a strong commitment to character-based hiring (character and competence) and communicates this expectation explicitly and frequently is in a better position than one who looks only at teaching credentials. During the interview of potential candidates for teaching positions, it would be advantageous to incorporate questions related to knowledge of character education as well as the candidate's character. Is the candidate's philosophy of education consistent with and supporting the school mission and touchstone? You might also develop a few ethical scenarios and ask for how they would respond.

One of the project districts was very explicit about the role of character in the hiring process. For new hires they used a character-based questionnaire from a commercial human resources firm. New staff knew from the beginning that character was important in this district.

It is also essential to orient new staff as to what expectations are in terms of professional and ethical behavior. Include in your orientation the school mission statement and touchstone and discuss how they are expected to also be the guiding principles in individual classrooms. Clearly define how the school functions and how to be a team player with not only their grade level or department, but with the entire school family. If your school uses peer mentors for first year teachers, insure that peer mentors are exemplary models of both character and instructional excellence.

Staff evaluation

Most principals have numerous items that they look for when evaluating staff, some of which are dictated contractually. If administrators have communicated that they expect good character to be modeled by staff, then assessments must include those elements. Without follow-up and accountability, staff will get the message that character is important only on paper, not in their everyday classroom life.

Our project offered administrators and staff a reflection tool developed by Dr. Matt Davidson for the *Smart & Good* project. The *Setting a Good Example* self-inventory below can be used by staff to reflect on how well they are modeling good character, as well as by administrators to communicate expectations to staff and use as a context to discuss with other assessments.

SETTING A GOOD EXAMPLE: A Faculty Self-Inventory

1. Do I come to class on time?
2. Am I well-prepared for class?
3. Do I return student work promptly?
4. Do I give individual comments that help students improve?
5. Do I treat students impartially and not show any kind of favoritism?
6. Do I take an interest in students and show concern when they experience problems at school or at home?
7. Do I maintain civility and graciousness with students even when under stress?
8. Do I model patience?
9. Do I refrain from speaking negatively about students in the faculty room and elsewhere? In speaking about students, do I exhibit the same respect I would want other teachers to show my own child?
10. Do I refrain from talking negatively to, or about, colleagues?
11. Do I model respect towards other teachers/staff and parents?
12. Do I hold out high expectations that challenge all my students to do their personal best?

Adapted from IEE/PELC self-inventory, Lickona & Davidson, 2005

Staff meetings

One of the biggest challenges our project faced, as do most schools, was that there was no time left in staff meetings to discuss character education. But, there does not need to be a lot of time given to this topic. It is very understandable that staff-meeting agendas are packed with many issues to be discussed; however, there is time to use reflective tools or checkpoint techniques to maintain the importance of good character. One strategy that was employed was to use quotes as a reflection tool for a 3-5 minute discussion. Or, to ask one staff member to share a practice he or she used to develop performance and moral character in their classroom. Some took a few minutes to discuss items from the "issue bin" to touch on practices that were and were not working. We also gave project schools a reflection tool based on *Uncommon*Sense™[17] to use as a five-minute warm-up in meetings. The "Honesty" is included below. What this does is communicate to staff that character is important to the school and that it needs to be actively, deliberately and regularly thought about and reflected on to be effective.

Staff recognition

There is always room for employee reward and recognition activities that help to build positive morale in the work environment. Think of staff recognition as a communication tool that reinforces and rewards the most important outcomes the staff creates for your school. When you recognize staff effectively, you reinforce, with your chosen means of recognition, the actions and behaviors you most want to see people repeat.

"A tree is known by its fruit; a man by his deeds. A good deed is never lost; he who sows courtesy reaps friendship, and he who plants kindness gathers love."

Saint Basil
Bishop of Cesarea

Recognizing publicly staff members who are making a positive difference takes little time but makes a significant impact. The recognition must be accompanied with specific information about what behaviors or actions are being rewarded and recognized in hopes others will follow. The simple words, "thank you" or "good job" shows your appreciation and support for hard work and contributions. A more gracious, polite workplace is appreciated by all, so model politeness and use the language that shows your sincerity.

One of the schools found success with "Pride Awards." Staff, parents or students could nominate staff for going "above and beyond." The nomination form asked why they thought this particular staff member deserved the award. At each staff meeting, nominations were read and later posted on a bulletin board in the hallway with the staff member's picture and their nomination form. Not only did staff feel appreciated and recognized, but they became an example to others.

*Uncommon*Sense®

Honesty

High character people speak the truth with compassion

Definition

"Ethical people speak up, present their facts with thoughtful accuracy, and do so with compassion. They are not avoiders; they are "care-fronters", they confront because they care. They clearly qualify their yes and no and thereby minimize misunderstandings. They do not deliberately mislead or deceive others by misrepresentations, overstatements, partial truths, selective omissions or other intentional means. They take responsibility and do not shift blame. To avoid confusing others, high character people break habits of sarcasm and cynicism. To avoid inflaming others, they avoid sanctimonious and condescending tones"

Activities/Reflections

1. Where would you place your self on the scale? Why? Think of a time in the past few weeks when you had too little honesty or too much.
2. Think about the last time you discovered a colleague was not honest with you. How did it make you feel? How did you react?
3. Think about the last time a colleague was too honest with you. How did it make you feel? How did you react?
4. Discuss with a partner "is it ever OK to tell a lie?"
5. Discuss with a partner ways to tell the truth with compassion. How do you want to hear the truth?
6. Select one of the quotes and discuss what it means to you with a partner or as a group.
7. Have you ever told the truth to someone and made the situation worse? What could you have done differently?

Too Little	Balanced	Too much
Vague	Truthful	Blunt
Deceptive	Straightforward	Harsh
Manipulative	Discrete	Brutal
Dishonest		Crude
Shady		
Liar		
Tricky		

Quotes

A half truth is a whole lie. *~Yiddish Proverb*

Who lies for you will lie against you. *~Bosnian Proverb*

Those who think it is permissible to tell white lies soon grow color-blind. *~Austin O'Malley*

We tell lies when we are afraid... afraid of what we don't know, afraid of what others will think, afraid of what will be found out about us. But every time we tell a lie, the thing that we fear grows stronger. *~Tad Williams*

People who are brutally honest get more satisfaction out of the brutality than out of the honesty. *~Richard J. Needham*

The highest compact we can make with our fellow is - "Let there be truth between us two forevermore." *~Ralph Waldo Emerson*

Our lives improve only when we take chances - and the first and most difficult risk we can take is to be honest with ourselves *~ Walter Anderson*

BBB The Center for Character Ethics

Notes

16. See http://www.characterandcitizenship.org/programs/leadershipacademy.htm for more information on the UMSL Center for Character and Citizenship's Leadership Academy for Character Education.

17. See http://centerforcharacterethics.org/resources/uncommonsense-framework for UncommonSense in its entirety.

5

Building Relationships

Relationships are the foundation for character education

Building relationships lays a foundation for developing a positive school climate and developing trust among staff to facilitate openness to professional development and change. One of the biggest obstacles the project had to overcome was the attitude that character education was something extra, something outside the classroom, and that it involved planning big "events" or service projects. We, project leaders and character coaches, needed to build relationships with staff so they would be open to the changes we were asking them to make. Helping staff understand that character education requires teachers and staff to self-reflect on, and perhaps change their behavior or their instructional methods and classroom management, can only occur in an atmosphere of mutual trusting relationships. Concurrently, we asked staff to build relationships with each other as well as with students and parents to lay the foundation for a positive school climate. We share some strategies and tools to build relationships below.

Tips for Building Relationships

Expressing yourself clearly is fundamental in building relationships as well as creating an unambiguous environment. The following guidelines that were designed to facilitate the workings of groups also apply to building relationships. Use them for self-reflection and guidance to insure your thoughts and ideas are skillfully expressed.

- **Be specific, not vague.** Use specific language to communicate what you think and feel to others, do not assume the listener will visualize the same picture that you have.
- **Communicate observations, not inferences.** Inferences go beyond what you have observed and make assumptions about what you think and feel, which can lead to misunderstandings.
- **Share ideas, not advice.** Avoid the tendency to evaluate and give advice to others, rather communicate the sharing of ideas and alternatives.
- **Communicate what was said, not why it was said.** Try not to assess motive or reasoning behind what another person says, focus your communication on observable information introduced by such words as what, how, when, and where.
- **Match nonverbal and verbal communication.** Try to match your voice, body, and gestures with the content of your verbal message to avoid mixed messages.

Your ability and willingness to send clear messages when you interact with others is essential to building relationships and working effectively in groups. To share information, opinions, and feelings in specific nonthreatening ways will enable you to communicate clearly and invite others to share more openly with you.

Source: *Creating Effective Groups* by Randy Fujishin

Strategies for positive staff-staff relationships

One of the most important elements of a healthy work relationship is trust. It is essential that school leaders and staff develop trust in order to accomplish goals. We found that at the beginning of the year, spending time to build relationships and strengthen bonds is crucial to the success of the character education initiative and building a positive school climate. People in every workplace talk about building the team and working as a team, but few understand how to develop an effective team. Fostering staff relationships means creating a work culture that values collaboration. Most schools, particularly high schools, operate in content "silos," with relatively little sharing among staff members except within content areas, and not always there. In a teamwork environment, people understand and believe that thinking, planning, decisions and actions are better when done cooperatively. People recognize and assimilate the belief that "none of us is as good as all of us." In order to achieve this ideal situation, the staff has to feel connected with each other and develop open and honest communication. Creating a positive work environment takes work. The following strategies were implemented successfully in the project.

1. **Holiday gatherings:** most schools have some type of holiday celebrations either as all adult gatherings out of school or in-school events. One school created a staff Thanksgiving party as a project for a special education class. The teacher worked with students to plan, cook, and serve a special Thanksgiving meal to all staff. There were three "seatings" that corresponded to the three teacher lunch periods. Not only did the staff get to share a special meal together, but the students learned everything that went into meal planning, cooking and serving.
2. **Games:** at prom time, one high school staff posted pictures of their own prom pictures in the teacher's lounge to see how many could identify them. The staff had a great time with this activity!
3. **Socialization opportunities:** One Friday a month, staff at one school had a breakfast potluck to socialize and get to know each other. Another school met one Friday a month at a local restaurant for happy hour (after school hours!) Neither of these activities took much planning, and helped staff get to know each other a little better.
4. **Faculty council:** At one high school where there had been a lot of staff divisiveness and frequent administrative turnover, the principal created a faculty council. He chose teachers so that each department and grade level was represented. The purpose of the group was to address problems that arose, so that teachers were solution-creators, rather than simply problem-finders. The council did not meet regularly but

instead met only when necessary. One topic this group addressed was field trips and the problems that often arise: student absences, last-minute notice, and loss of instructional time. The principal explained that until they created an appropriate solution, there would be no field trips. The council quickly devised their plan. This required compromise, but staff felt they had a "voice" in the decision that was made. Besides developing and nurturing relationships, this opportunity also allowed teachers to take ownership of their actions and student learning.

5. **Social Committee:** some schools had a formal social committee of staff that planned social events (not just to recognize birthdays). Examples included game nights, potlucks, sports teams, tailgating before school games, treasure hunts, and mixers between buildings.
6. **"Teachers Playbook":** A sports-minded principal at one high school created the opportunity for staff to improve relationships through sharing best practices. Staff would offer to share a particular topic or strategy that might be of interest to other staff. Some of the topics included internet resources for helping students to organize their thoughts and essays, helpful video sites, and hands-on organizers. Typically, 10-15 staff members attended. The group brainstormed ideas to increase attendance and decided to have several topics ready in advance and staff would "sign up" at the beginning of the year, both to present and to attend.
7. **Sharing:** One school invited staff twice a month to get together over lunch or common planning time to share best/new practices.
8. **Student trainers:** One school trained a student leadership team in asset building. That group of students then led staff in the team building activities they had learned.

"The quality of teacher-student relationships is the keystone for all other aspects of classroom management."

Marzano and Marzano, Dimensions of Learning

Strategies for positive staff-student relationships

Most staff understands the need to develop positive relationships with students, but all can benefit from new ideas to make their efforts more intentional. The following are some strategies that were utilized to enhance staff/student relationships.

School-wide activities

1. **Character café:** One of the high schools began a character café as a way to recognize students. Their goal was to acknowledge students who demonstrated a good work ethic, attitude and other character and

leadership qualities. Students who were recommended by at least three teachers for exemplary character were invited to a luncheon. The teachers prepared or provided the food and gathered with the students to enjoy the good food and laughter. Students looked forward to this event and were thrilled when they are chosen to attend. The teachers also baked favorite treats for students to share during testing weeks.

2. **Care Team:**[18] One of the schools found success with a "Care Team." Care Teams are comprised of teachers and community resource members such as police officers, social workers, and juvenile court representatives. The purpose of the Care Team was to assist schools and communities in developing partnerships among and with other organizations for the well-being of students and families. The Care Team met regularly to assess student and family needs for students that might not be receiving services, or were in danger of "falling through the cracks." The benefits of the Care Team were better communications; sharing of expertise and resources within the Care Team, with the school and families and throughout the school district; development of collaborative interventions to identify and find resolutions to meet all student needs; and implementation of clearly defined prevention, intervention and education services to promote student success and positive relationships. For example, at one meeting they discussed a student whose grades had slipped and seemed headed for trouble. It was discussed that this student was experiencing a difficult family situation. One teacher brought up the student's interest in art, and another teacher volunteered to have the student stay after school with him to help him in the art room.

Collaboration
Assets
Relationships
Engaged Learning

"Our team gathers for a purpose. IT IS A COMMUNITY EFFORT! For approximately one hour, weekly, this committed group meets to make a difference in children's lives. The focus of their conversation: those students who are struggling academically and socially, those students who have minimal support, and those who suffer with ongoing discipline problems. Experts throughout the county, along with school staff, share information, discuss attributing factors, and generate ideas for helping each student. Together a goal is established and progress is monitored weekly."

Care Team leader

3. **Advisory:** Many schools already have some form of advisory or homeroom periods. Whether they use it to intentionally build relationships or to further performance and moral character development, varies. One of our schools had an existing advisory program at the high school that had regular activities to help students get to know each other. Another middle school had time built into the day for a "homeroom" at the beginning of the school day, but no required activities. The character coach developed a resource of team-building and character-developing activities that staff could use during this period. Another school spent a year researching effective advisory programs and was able to implement it during the final year of the project.
4. **Staff-student activities:** One school organized a staff- student basketball game that was held after school and used to raise money for a service project.
5. **Pride Awards:** Teachers would nominate students for Pride Awards that were given monthly. This is different from "student of the month" because it is not limited to one or two students. We discouraged the traditional "student of the month" programs because they didn't give all students the opportunity to achieve recognition for their character and behavior. By recognizing all students who displayed good character (or compassion, helpfulness, etc.) each month, everyone has a chance to be recognized, not just 10-15 students a year.

Building relationships begins with how we treat others, what we say and how we say it.

6. **"Schoolmanship" dog tags:** One middle school created a set of "dog tags" that were used as rewards for various accomplishments. The "schoolmanship" tags were awarded for students "caught" doing the right thing without being asked, or showing pride in their school. Other tags were awarded for honor roll, perfect attendance, extra effort, zero infractions, birthdays, and one for learning the school touchstone.

7. **Extra-curricular activities and affinity groups:** One middle school organized a series of "girl groups" to reach girls who didn't necessarily participate in other school activities. Their purpose was to help each age group make positive adjustments to school and deal with pressures of adolescence. The box below describes how these groups were organized and operated.

GEMS

Girl Empowerment Meetings

GEMS is for sixth grade girls to offer support and mentoring during their first year at the middle school. This is a voluntary group that meets on Fridays during the sixth grade lunch period.

GAPP

Girls Are Powerful People

GAPP is a group of seventh grade girls who voluntarily meet during their lunch periods on Fridays to participate in various community service projects. Their projects range from hosting teacher appreciation luncheons, serving at soup kitchens, helping with Red Cross Blood Drives, caring for animals at the Humane Society, facilitating canned food drives, and offering free babysitting to the community during the Christmas season.

GAMMA

Girls Are Mentoring and Maturing Altogether

The eighth grade GAMMA Girls meet on Fridays during their lunch periods. The goals of GAMMA Girls are to mentor younger girls to adjusting to middle school, to make good choices, to form healthy relationships, and to develop a positive self-image. They give classroom presentations, chat with the sixth grade GEMS group, promote positive behaviors on the morning announcements, facilitate a babysitting clinic, and visit the elementary school to build relationships with the fifth grade girls to help educate them about the effects of relational aggression (i.e., girl bullying) and ways to overcome negative behaviors and interactions.

> "We cannot teach students well if we do not know them well."
>
> **Hoffman and Leak**

Strategies for staff

One school asked staff to reflect and be intentional in their attempts to build relationships with students. They asked each staff member to complete the following form at a staff meeting:

Action Planning and Commitment Form

Name ____________________

School ____________________

Position ____________________

1. A. I can do the following tomorrow to strengthen and enhance my **RELATIONSHIPS** with students.

   B. I can implement the following longer range ideas to strengthen and enhance my **RELATIONSHIPS** with students.

2. A. I can do the following within the next week to create an ASSET-RICH **ENVIRONMENT** in the halls, in my classroom, or before and after school.

   B. I can implement the following longer range ideas to create an ASSET-RICH **ENVIRONMENT** in the halls, in my classroom, or before and after school.

3. I can integrate Developmental Assets in my current **CURRICULUM**. (Name lesson/s.)

4. I recognize these opportunities to strengthen and expand asset building through my **INSTRUCTIONAL PRACTICES**.

5. Look back at all your ideas above. Draw a box around any ideas that you will commit to doing.

Signature ____________________ Date ____________________

Once staff had generated ideas on how they could improve relationships with students and committed doing at least a few, it was important to follow up. This school had teachers report out every few months on what they had implemented and their progress. Without follow up and accountability, staff quickly learn that they don't need to make any changes.

One of the most effective ways for staff to build relationships with students is via their classroom behavior and instructional methods. Middle and high school students are keenly attuned to whether they think a teacher cares about them. One school created a rule that they must all say "Good morning" to a student first, because there were too many, "Tuck in your shirt, pull up those pants, where are you supposed to be" comments from teachers first thing in the morning. Another school created a rule that they must give out five positive referrals before they could write a discipline referral. This forced teachers to focus on the positive rather than the negative. All of our project schools encouraged staff to actively engage students in learning. In the classroom strategies section (Chapter 8), we provide numerous examples of strategies that can be used in the classroom to promote active participation by students.

Developing relationships with students requires understanding or trying to get to know them. One school used the following "acknowledgement ticket" for staff to reach out to the students:

> *What a Great Teen!*
>
> **Ways to Build Assets and Tell a Teen They are Valued**
>
> This coupon is for: Lunch with the faculty member of your choice (our treat!)
>
> Student____

How do you know if your efforts to build relationships are successful? There are a number of indicators that students have positive relationships with their teacher, such as:

- Classroom/teacher evaluations show that the students feel the teacher cares about them.
- Class attendance improves.
- Student participation increases.
- Parents are responsive and feel connected to their child's learning.

These indicators can be measured formally with surveys or informally anecdotally, but it is important to assess progress to know if you are having an impact.

Strategies for positive student relationships

Fostering positive relationships among students is one of the most difficult goals to accomplish because of the physical, emotional and social challenges of adolescence. The cliques and social angst of middle and high school can create havoc and lead to bullying and physical fighting. Anytime a teacher can create a teamwork environment, students will have more opportunity to collaborate and work together. Our schools employed a number of strategies to encourage positive student relationships, among them:

1. **Affirmation assignment:** One school integrated this assignment (developed by Hal Urban) in their Language Arts curriculum. During their study of poetry, they used it to build positive relationships among their students and encouraged them to talk to classmates they didn't usually talk to.

> "Words go into the body. They can cause us to be well and hopeful and happy and high-energy and wondrous and funny and cheerful." **Maya Angelou**
>
> **Assignment:** Use your words to make someone else feel one of the things Maya Angelou mentions above. Give three people a verbal affirmation—one that is personal, not physical (hair, clothes, looks, etc.). Make someone feel good.
>
> Person: ____________________
>
> Relationship: ____________________
>
> What you said: ____________________
>
> ____________________
>
> ____________________
>
> ____________________
>
> Response: ____________________
>
> ____________________
>
> ____________________
>
> ____________________
>
> From Hal Urban, *Lessons from the Classroom*

2. **Classroom grouping:** Teachers employed a variety of grouping techniques in the classroom, some of them random. Using a variety of strategies does not allow the same students to be grouped together and leads to more engagement and interaction. It is good to mix it up occasionally. One middle school utilized anti-bullying techniques they had learned at an in-service to seat students in the classroom according to whether the student was a potential bully, victim or bystander.
3. **Service learning projects:** Working together on service projects helps students learn more about each other and develop empathy. All of our schools participated in numerous service activities and encouraged all students to participate. A key concept here is to communicate the expectation that all students participate in some way, and to offer both service to the school and service to the community. True service learning, where the service activity is intentionally infused in the curriculum (the learning part) is more difficult to accomplish; one of our schools developed a comprehensive service learning program concurrently with their character project, the goals of which overlapped and complemented each other.
4. **Cooperative learning opportunities:** Most teachers are aware of cooperative learning techniques; however we provided some professional development on ways to train students to work productively in groups. Teachers must insure that each student on a team has a fundamental role and a responsibility to the team. Developing relationships and trust among group members is essential to successful groups.
5. **Laws of Life Essay Contest:** One school used the contest as a way to help both teachers and students to get to know each other as well as develop empathy for each other. The contest also meets the 4 Keys criteria for "public performance" thus it is a valuable tool in a character education program. For more information and free resources about the contest go to http://lol.centerforcharacterethics.org

Strategies for positive relationships with parents and community

Positive relationships among staff and parents are integral to the success of the educational structure for students. Parents are the primary and most important moral educators of their children. Thus, public schools should develop character education programs in close partnership with parents and the community. Garnering parent and community support early in the process and including them in the selection of shared values is critical to avoiding pushback.

Staff must make every effort to keep all lines of communication open. Communication with parents can take place in various ways. The following strategies were useful methods in communicating with parents:

1. **Phone calls home:** Teachers that made continuous effort to call parents throughout the year with positive words about the students had far better parental relationships compared to the teachers that called home for negative reasons alone. Although it is important to communicate with parents for academic or behavioral concerns, it is equally important to communicate for positive reasons. Some schools required teachers to make a certain number of calls a week, of which a certain number had to be positive.
2. **Invitations by phone to attend conferences:** Middle and high schools often have difficulty getting parents to attend conferences, so a personal invitation can help improve the odds of parents attending.
3. **Positive postcards home:** Several schools employed this method of communicating with parents with positive comments to say about their child.
4. **"Student publicity":** Some schools went to great lengths to highlight student accomplishments in local newspapers, school newsletters, and on school websites.
5. **Parent Academy:** One of the biggest successes was enjoyed by one high school that invited parents to "Parent Academy" night. They provided a simple dinner (hot dogs), and babysitting (student groups). Parents attended "classes" that explained the curriculum their students would be learning. It wasn't the typical "meet the teacher" night, but rather ways to help their students learn and how to follow their progress. With technologies such as "Progress Book" (a software program used by many districts to track school and classroom data and information), many schools have rich resources for parents to see what their teens are learning and learn strategies to help them. Structuring the meeting in this way, this school saw double the attendance than they usually had at parent meetings.

Notes

18. Learn more about Care Teams at http://www.mvesc.k12.oh.us/5

6

Staff Development

Staff development for character education initiatives is a re-orientation and a fresh way of looking and approaching common issues; it often has a problem-solving aspect to it. Schools can start slow, choosing to add new activities each year. Much of what a school chooses to implement is self-governed; each school chooses what they want based on their particular needs and resources. For example, one school in our project ascertained that they had a bullying problem so they researched programs and decided that the *Olweus*[19] program best met their needs. They then scheduled professional development on how to implement that program. Another school selected the "Top Twenty"[20] program and scheduled several after school and summer trainings.

In our project multiple ways of approaching staff development were utilized and they are discussed below.

In-house whole-staff orientations and trainings

Many districts start their year with an "all-staff" training or orientation. We had one school that was able to schedule this type of training, bringing in the developer of the model to address all staff. For major new initiatives, this is an effective and efficient way to orient staff to the project and teach them new concepts. However, keep in mind that a "one and done" approach doesn't last—without additional efforts to engage staff in training or professional development, the impact of a single training is reduced.

In-service training days

Another school scheduled a session during one of their regularly scheduled in-service days to introduce the project to another school. Again, this is a good strategy to introduce a new project, but without help or follow-up, impact fades.

Built-in planning time

One of the most effective means of staff development is to schedule it during built in planning time. One school had scheduled regular planning time each day before school. Some days were designated for department meetings, some for grade level, and some for other committee meetings. They used this time period on a regular basis to introduce and provide more depth for staff on the project (for example, using the 4 Keys).

Outside training with reporting in

Most schools have some funds to send staff to outside trainings or conferences. These are important because the intensity of an outside training (think immersion) is much greater than an in-house training with the distractions of daily life. But, few schools effectively utilize the investment they have made in that staff member. If staff attend conferences or outside training, there needs to be some reporting out procedure where they can share what they have learned. One idea is to use the model mastery approach described below.

Skill-building on targeted subjects

The examples of specific skill-building discussed at the beginning of the chapter illustrate this strategy. This seemed to be the strategy of choice for most schools in the project; most selected a program or topic they wanted to "go deep" on and brought in trainers or sent staff for in-depth training. Because this usually involves a greater cost in time and money, it is important that options be carefully researched so that the new program will meet the school's needs. There also needs to be staff buy-in so that all commit to implementation. Schools that took time to research a program, "sell" it to the entire staff and implement over time were most successful.

Rotating half-day training

One school used this strategy to orient and train all staff at the beginning of the project. The character coach scheduled substitutes to free each staff member for a half day. Half the staff attended the workshop in the morning and half attended in the afternoon. Thereby one substitute could cover for 2 staff members (actually more counting free periods). She planned a series of activities, handouts, and discussions so that each staff member learned the key concepts (for example performance and moral character and the 4 Keys) of the project. This maximized the impact (all staff participated) with half the number of substitutes. This strategy could also be used to do more in-depth training on particular strategies, using in-house experts or consultants. A sample half-day schedule for introducing the *Smart & Good* concepts is included below.

Character Education Professional Development Workshop

1. Introduction: Show "The Teddy Stallard Story" (www.makeadifferencemovie.com), a fictional but moving account of how teachers can make a difference.
2. The 4 Keys: Giving maximum power to the classroom
   a. Adopt or adapt lesson plans (*Smart & Good* Report, p.29)
   b. Ron Berger/ "Creating a Culture of Excellence: 5 Pedagogical Practices" (S&G, p.50)
3. The English Teacher Raises the Bar (S&G p. 107)
   a. Activity—Identify 4 Keys in this teacher's approach to teaching reading.
   b. Q—Which of the 8 strengths of character is this teacher forming in her students?
   c. Share how you use one of the 4 Keys in your classroom.
4. Break
5. Promising Practices: Using rubrics
   a. Effort rubric (S&G p.109)
      i. How is this rubric a "self-study"?
      ii. How can it be an "other study"?
      iii. What kind of "public performance" can come from this rubric?
      iv. How can your classroom be a "community that supports and challenges"?
   b. Leader to detractor rubric (S&G p.111)
      i. Adopt or adapt?
      ii. Using common language in all classrooms (Are you a 5 or a 1?)

"Whatever job you are asked to do, do a good one—because your reputation is your résumé."

Madeline Albright

Thank you for your time today!

Model mastery

Schools that cannot afford to hire instructional coaches can often achieve a similar result using the "model mastery" approach. Schools identify a teacher of best practices from each grade level and/or subject to model effective strategies and techniques throughout the school or department (or district) for their grade and subject level. The teacher must be able and willing to model strategies in other classrooms as well as be exemplars of good character (character and competence). They should be a master teacher of best practices in teaching strategies and techniques, a teacher who can demonstrate methods of delivering information with a meaningful approach, and a teacher that uses the development of performance and moral character to enhance instruction and learning. It also requires a teacher who is well-respected by other staff and has good relationships with them. Once the model teacher has been identified, school administrators use available resources to schedule an extra free period for them or find a substitute to free him/her for a day on a regular basis to allow them to demonstrate exemplary practices in other classrooms. In our project, the character coaches served in this capacity. Not all staff are open to inviting another staff member into their classrooms, so it is important that the administration emphasizes that this is not a reflection of poor performance, but rather a way for all staff to improve and share effective practices. Different staff models can be used to demonstrate different practices—especially if school funds have been invested in special training for a particular staff member. The maximum "return" on this investment is to have these trained staff demonstrate to, and work with, other staff to help them implement the new techniques.

Professional learning communities (PLC)

PLC's have become very common strategies for professional development and most of our schools utilized them to some extent. There are numerous resources on forming PLC's (see for example Richard Dufour's books on the subject). We asked our project schools to add "ethical" to the PLC's goals—that is, they were asked to align everything they did to the school touchstone and the goals of excellence and ethics.[21]

Visual reminders

Everyone needs reminders and "refreshers" to stay the course because change does not happen overnight. During our second year of implementation we provided every staff member with a half-sheet of heavy paper to which we attached a small toy compass (available inexpensively from novelty websites). On the card we printed the quote in the box below, to hopefully inspire and remind staff of the importance of their role in influencing the lives of their students and in the success for the project.

Be the Compass in Your School

There are so many children who come to our schools who will experience the best part of their day under our care. For some students we are the first person who has spoken to them that day. For others, our smiling faces and food in the cafeteria are the first and perhaps only sustenance they will receive that day. For other children, we are the people who give them hugs, spend time with them, help them with their problems and even worry about them when they are away from us. For some children we are their model. They love their parents but still look to us to help guide them and be an example to them. In essence, we are their *moral compass*. Please take these compasses and place them on your desk. Every morning before the children come into your classroom, take a moment to look at the compass and reflect that today we have the opportunity by our words and examples to show students that true north is a worthwhile pursuit.

from a North Carolina principal, as re-told by Phil Vincent, Character Development Group

Notes

19. See http://www.violencepreventionworks.org/public/index.page
20. See http://www.top20training.com/
21. See Chapter 3 in the *Smart & Good High Schools* report (2005) for suggestions on how this type of school professional development can operate.

7

School-Wide Strategies for Creating a Positive School Climate and Developing Performance and Moral Character

Creating a positive school climate and developing performance and moral character takes intentional and deliberate action; rarely does it happen on its own. There are many books and articles about school climate[22] and many strategies that can be pursued. While our primary focus was on changing the classroom culture, we did encourage school-wide strategies that helped build relationships and create a positive atmosphere in the school and that helped foster student character development. In reality, most all the strategies implemented during the project contributed to school climate; we highlight some that were particularly salient in this chapter.

Welcoming atmosphere

One of the most important components of positive school climate is to create a welcoming atmosphere. Students and parents need to feel that the staff knows who they are, will listen to them and value them. This should be the simplest school improvement strategy because it requires no training or cost—but it is often the most difficult because it requires a change in attitude and behavior on the part of staff (see quote on following page).

All of our project schools implemented strategies to create a more welcoming atmosphere. For example, at one middle school, the principal started a monthly parent book club. The school had seen a decline in attendance at parent organization meetings as do many middle schools; parents of middle school students often become less involved. To entice them back, she selected books relevant to parents of adolescents—titles such as *Fires in the Bathroom*.[23] Unlike previous parent meetings which attracted fewer than a handful of parents, 40-60 parents met every six weeks to discuss several chapters and the challenges of this age group. Parents connected with each other as well as the principal and some of the staff that attended. By discussing the parenting and educational challenges this age group presents, they created a feeling that, "we are all in the same boat." Rather than asking parents to come to school to participate in fundraising activities, she listened to their concerns and took action to address them.

> "I remember a school I observed years ago that wanted to create a more welcoming atmosphere, so they asked the PTA to purchase a pair of wicker chairs, a small area rug, table, and potted plant. They arranged a cozy sitting area at the entrance to the school. They assumed that if the school *looked* welcoming, it would *be* welcoming. It didn't work. No one acted any differently and parents still didn't feel as if they were welcome at the school."
>
> **Educational consultant**

A major initiative at all our schools was to encourage (some even required) teachers to greet students at the door of the classroom each period. Hal Urban, teacher, author and national speaker recommends this strategy in his book *Lessons from the Classroom* (see Chapter 8 for more about Hal Urban). The simple act of personally greeting each student to the classroom each day, not only welcomes students, but also models appropriate business behavior—looking someone in the eye, shaking their hand and speaking to them by name. Each student gets the message, "The teacher knows who I am and that I matter." Again, this is simple, costless and easy—but it was surprisingly difficult to get teachers to adopt. But, with concerted effort and frequent reminders, we began to see more of this behavior over the course of the project.

It is also important to include all staff, not just teaching staff, in this re-orientation to creating a positive school atmosphere. Office staff are usually the first person parents see when they enter a building, so warm, welcoming and helpful office staff is essential. Custodians, cafeteria workers and bus drivers also need training on the goals of character education and the role they play in creating a positive and safe climate.

Service projects

As discussed in the previous chapters, service learning and character education are a natural fit. Service projects help build relationships and give students an opportunity for "moral action"—one of the Character Education Partnership's *Eleven Principles of Effective Character Education* (see www.character.org to access this publication). Most schools have some type of service projects. Service projects can also satisfy one of the 4 Keys—public performance. Service projects require students to be responsible—for jobs such as collecting and delivering food to the needy, mentoring younger students, helping senior citizens, or cleaning and beautifying school grounds. All of these tasks challenge students to do their best and be their best, because someone else is depending on them; lessons not easily learned elsewhere.

Advisories

Advisories were discussed in Chapter 5 as great ways to build relationships between and among students and staff. Thoughtful planning for advisories can also promote a positive school climate. In too many schools, advisories are the place to pass out papers and catch up on homework.

One high school decided to implement an advisory program. They formed a committee of interested staff, spent a year planning and researching advisories, provided staff development on how to implement what they selected, and set expectations that all staff were to participate.

They created a series of activities for advisory periods that were grade specific, and incorporated service learning, character development goals, career and college planning, and some study skills. Used in this manner, advisory can meet a number the goals of multiple initiatives. The schedule on the following page gives topics for each grade level each month, covering the multiple purposes it was designed to address. They also developed lessons and resources for each topic that were distributed to advisory staff.

Recognizing the importance of reflection to the development of performance and moral character, they also developed a reflection tool for students to use that helped provide feedback on the activities they participated in, which is included on page 67. They used student and staff feedback to revise the lessons and topic schedule over the summer each year.

Advisor/Advisee Schedule				
	9th Grade Study Skills	**10th Grade Career Planning**	**11th Grade PS Options**	**12th Grade "Experience"**
August	Getting to Know You	All About Me	Getting to Know You	Getting to Senioritis
September	Service-Learning Plan	Service-Learning Plan	Service-Learning Plan	Service-Learning Plan
September	Time Management	Myself and Me Alone	College Degree Options	College Applications
October	Interim Grades Goal-Setting	Interim Grades Communication Skills	Interim Grades (Review SL focus)	Interim Grades Financial Aid
October	What Helps Me Learn	What Employers Look for	College Planning	The Art of Conversation
November	Respect for Others	Ways You Show Respect	E-mail Etiquette (ACT/Compass testing?)	Second Semester Issues
November	World of Work	Career Action Steps	Top Ten Soft Skills	Speaker
December	Interim Grades Select Your Courses	Interim Grades CAS continued	Openness	Reflection on Speaker FAFSA
January	Scheduling (counselors) Holiday Stereotyping	Scheduling (counselors)	Scheduling (counselors) Openness continued	Interviews
April	Excuses, Excuses (Integrity)	Excuses, Excuses (Integrity)	Professional Etiquette	Speaker
April	Take Control of Homework	Circles of My MC Self	PS Vocabulary	Speaker Reflection Mock Interview
May	Reflections Advisory and SL	Reflections Advisory and SL	Reflections Advisory and SL	Reflections Advisory and SL

Note to teachers: These lessons are guides. Please feel free to modify any to fit the needs of your students. If you discover a better lesson, please share it!

Advisory Reflection

Name ______________________________ Grade Level ____________

Take a few minutes to revisit the various topics you and your classmates discussed during advisory this year.

1. Which topic was most beneficial to you? Why?
2. Which topic was least beneficial to you? Why?
3. If you were to suggest one topic not to include next year, what would it be? Why? Which topic(s) would you include instead of that one?
4. Reflect on your service-learning project. What part did you take in the project? How did you "grow" by participating in the project?

School-wide and motivational assemblies

Although we have stressed that motivational assemblies are not necessary for good character education to take place, some schools find them useful as ways to build a positive school climate, particularly as a way to kick off the school year, as mid-year reminders or as a reward for accomplishments. They do not, however, take the place of positive relationships and the other strategies that have been discussed so far. One school used local football "heroes" who talked to students about how their character contributed to their success. They talked about how persistence, hard work, making good choices, and respect for others helped them achieve success on the football field as well as in life. Positive role models that students can identify with (as having similar backgrounds) helped introduce the messages that the school was trying to emphasize. The key was the participation and follow-up by staff. They developed lessons that they used in their advisory period to help students reflect on what they had heard and use it to set goals for themselves.

Another school had a series of quarterly "State of the School" assemblies. At these, the principal discussed the accomplishments of each class in terms of attendance, discipline referrals, and grades. Other accomplishments such as service projects were also recognized. The class with the best "numbers" was awarded custody of the school "spirit stick" which was theirs to hold on to or lose at the next assembly. This vehicle for school and class pride served as a reminder of what was expected on a regular basis, with a little competition built in to make it fun for the students.

School grading policies

Two schools in the project made changes to their grading policies to reflect their new emphasis on performance and moral character. To be aligned, grading must encourage and reward effort and motivation and encourage students to do their best work. Including an assessment of character communicates to students and parents that behavior and character matter and that students will be held accountable.

How does the school grading policy influence student behavior and learning? Dr. Lickona provides the following assessment tool to assist schools that want to evaluate their grading system:

Grading Policy Assessment

1. How does the grading policy impact student motivation to learn, improve, and other aspects of performance character? Is an effort rubric used, for example, to foster that aspect of performance character?
2. Does the grading policy encourage a minority of students (who get top grades) but discourage others? What do students say about that?
3. Does the system recognize improvement (as in an Honor Roll for students who improve their average by a certain number of points?)
4. Does the grading system keep some students from taking tough classes because they don't want to jeopardize their class rank (which some schools have abolished in order to deemphasize the kind of competition that puts the focus on grades rather than learning)?
5. Do the grading approaches used by teachers give precise enough/frequent enough feedback to spur and assist students' revision of their work to higher levels of excellence?
6. Do teachers use the 4 KEYS to help students take responsibility for their grades and learn strategies for improving them?
7. How does the grading policy contribute to, or undermine, academic integrity? Is the grading policy, whatever it is, coupled with multiple strategies, including an honor code and school touchstone, to foster a culture of integrity?

Source: Dr. Thomas Lickona

One school revised their entire report card formats for the middle and high school. They, they identified four "life skills" they wished to assess—attendance and timeliness, work ethic, responsibility and respectfulness, and "quality producer." Each quality was assessed on a 0-4 scale. The rubric on pages 70-71 shows how they did this.

The first three life skills were added to the middle school report card and students received a grade (0-4) for each life skill for each subject. In the high school, all four life skills were used, but instead of separate grades on each in each subject, they were counted as 10% of the grade in each class.

The Power of ICU

The *Power of ICU*, by principals Danny Hill and Dr. Jayson Nave,[24] gives wonderful information and insight on how to transform current grading practices to reflect students' true ability and not let students slip through the cracks. It is a "no-zeros" grading system that aims at holding students accountable and decreasing student apathy. One project school adopted this program, received training and tracked progress. Students were expected to complete all assignments and they received an "I" (incomplete) for work not finished—but all assignments had to be completed. They developed a rewards, incentive and consequences policy to motivate students. And, to provide academic support, they added a daily, one hour "extra help" period for all students by reducing all periods by five minutes and creating in essence a "common study hall." During that period, students could seek help from any of their teachers and re-do assignments. Teachers could re-teach and provide interventions for students. The results were immediate—the number of failures on report cards decreased by 87% and in addition, the number of disciplinary incidents decreased by 64%!

LIFE SKILLS ASSESSMENT RUBRIC

Attendance/Timeliness: Present and/or on time for learning

Work Ethic: Prepared for and engaged in learning

Responsible/Respectful: Works independently and cooperatively; respects others and property

Quality Producer: Recognizes and produces quality products and performances

KEY: 4—Outstanding; exemplary
3—Satisfactory
2—Needs Improvement
1—Habits interfere with achievement
0—No evidence

The following is a description for each of the above approaches to learning:

ATTENDANCE/TIMELINESS: Present and/or on time for learning

4 Student has excellent attendance and is on time to class.

3 Student could improve attendance; is sometimes tardy.

2 Student has attendance and/or tardy problem that disrupts learning.

1 Student has habitual attendance problem that is interfering with academic achievement; often comes late to class without an excuse.

0 Severe problems with attendance and/or tardiness.

WORK ETHIC: Completes assigned work; prepared/participates in class

4 Student is punctual or early in completing and turning in assignments; often participates in classroom activities/discussions; consistently prepared for class and has needed supplies.

3 Student usually completes and turns in assignments on time; sometimes participates in classroom activities/discussions; prepared for class most of the time and usually brings supplies.

2 Student often fails to complete and turn in assignments on time; rarely participates in classroom activities/discussions; often unprepared for class and does not bring needed supplies.

1 Student fails to complete and turn in assignments; does not participate in classroom activities/discussions; not prepared for class and neglects to bring needed supplies

0 No evidence of being prepared for learning.

LIFE SKILLS ASSESSMENT RUBRIC (con't)

RESPONSIBLE/RESPECTFUL: Works both independently and cooperatively; respects others and privacy

4 Student is consistently responsible, uses self-control, is reliable and self-reliant when working independently; actively listens and consistently follows classroom rules and procedures; consistently works cooperatively and demonstrates respect for others; uses good manners; is considerate of others and tolerant of differences; consistently respectful of both personal and school property.

3 Student is responsible most times; uses self-control and is usually reliable when working independently; listens most of the time and follows classroom rules and procedures; usually works cooperatively and is respectful of others; usually exhibits good manners and gets along with others; usually respectful of both personal property and school property.

2 Student often lacks self-control, is unreliable and depends upon direction and assistance from others when working independently; does not listen well and often does not follow classroom rules and procedures; can be uncooperative and disrespectful of the differences of others and their points of view; exhibits poor manners and has trouble getting along with others; often disrespectful of and negligent in taking care of both personal and school property.

1 Student lacks self-control, is unreliable and often refuses direction and assistance from others when working independently; does not listen and refuses to follow classroom rules and procedures; is uncooperative and disrespectful of the differences of others and their points of view; lacks manners and does not get along with others; disrespectful of and negligent in taking care of both personal and school property.

0 No evidence of responsible or respectful behavior

QUALITY PRODUCER: Recognizes and produces quality products and performances

4 Student meets high expectations of quality; develops plans to complete projects of quality; develops high quality first drafts; critically analyzes own work; revises based on recommendations of self and others; persists until expectations are met.

3 Student attempts to meet high expectations of quality; timeline for completing projects are somewhat incomplete; first drafts are done but not of highest quality; lacks thoroughness in analyzing own work; does some revision from recommendations of self and others; continues working but final product not always thorough and complete.

2 Student has little concern about quality; fails to follow through on plans to complete projects of quality; first drafts are missing or of low quality; does not critically analyze own work or make revisions suggested by others; shows little or no persistence to produce high quality work.

1 Student shows no interest or persistence to produce work of quality

0 No evidence of quality

Notes

22. See for example Elbot, C. F., & Fulton, D.V. (2008). *Building an Intentional School Culture: Excellence in Academics and Character*. Thousand Oaks, CA: Corwin Press
23. Cushman, K. (2003). *Fires in the bathroom*. New York: The New Press.
24. Hill, D. & Nave, J. *Power of ICU*. (2009). NTLB Publishing the Educational Imprint of Southland Books.

8

Classroom Strategies

The key to success and sustainability of a character education program is whether it can impact classroom teaching. Many educators view character education as the "extras"—the assemblies, the posters on the wall, the "words of the month," and recognition programs such as "student of the month." In fact, one of the principals in the project, when asked how things were going the first year, replied, "Well, we haven't had much time to plan any events." Fortunately his staff had been busy integrating the 4 Keys and touchstone into their classrooms, and we placed a much greater emphasis on helping all principals the following year!

A great deal of time and professional development focused on bringing "excellence and ethics" into the classroom. We provided some training and resources, but we soon found that the "early adopters" were busy creating wonderful tools and resources in their classrooms. This chapter shares many of those tools and resources.

Rubrics

A major function of the rubrics that were shared, adapted or created was to help students self-reflect on their behavior, effort, knowledge or understanding. Rubrics also define what is expected at each level of accomplishment, so students know what the "path to excellence" is. Too many students don't produce quality work because they don't know what quality work looks like.[25] They also don't make the connection between working hard and better results. Regular use of rubrics can help students better understand their own work ethic and provide strategies for improvement. The following pages include numerous rubrics that can be used for this purpose.

Leader to Detractor Scale

This rubric appears on page 111 of the Smart & Good book. It was so useful that we are reprinting it here. The scale was created by a National School of Character winner, and used in the classroom for students to assess where they were functioning and to set goals for improvement. Once the scale is familiar to students, teachers can also use it to manage student behavior—asking "Are you being a 5 or a 1?"

One teacher developed rubrics for her classroom by combining the Leader to Detractor scale and the definition of performance and moral character. Students can self-assess, but it also helps both the student and teacher define and reinforce what those traits are.

After several years of trying these rubrics in some of the classrooms, this school adapted and adopted them to be included in their student planners, so all students and teachers could use them regularly (every nine weeks). The middle and high school version is shown on page 78. They also adapted them for use with elementary students (page 79).

LEADER TO DETRACTOR SCALE FOR LEVELS OF ACADEMIC FUNCTIONING **(ADAPTED from Lickona & Davidson, 2005, pg 111)**					
	Attendance, Preparedness & Attitude	**Healthy Habits of Learning**	**Demonstration of Learning**	**Intellectual Work Ethic**	**Role in Group Work**
Leader (5): Demonstrates personal commitment and mastery, and encourages others by word and deed to do the same.	Arrives on time with materials; functions with intensity and stamina; advances the goals of the class through personal contributions and by assisting others in these areas.	Demonstrates exemplary organization, time management, and excellent note-taking; demonstrates strong word-processing, reading and writing skills, actively assists others in these areas.	Demonstrates mastery of course requirements at highest level including ease and flexibility of using expected learner outcomes; assists others in these areas.	Demonstrates strong persistence, dedication, curiosity, and enthusiasm for individual academic pursuits, while encouraging the development of these qualities in others.	Demonstrates teamwork, initiative, and willingness to work, with others demonstrates the ability to organize and lead group toward stated goals, but also does his/her part in the actual group tasks; encourages teamwork and leadership in others.
Participant (3): Carries out responsibilities in an adequate way, but does not take on a leadership role.	Arrives on time with materials; functions adequately—not leading, but not detracting	Demonstrates adequate organization and time management, note-taking, word-processing, reading and writing skills—not leading others, but not detracting either.	Demonstrates adequate mastery of course requirements, and some facility and flexibility in using expected learner outcomes—not leading others, but not detracting either.	Demonstrates adequate (i.e., lacking intensity and consistency) persistence, dedication, curiosity, and enthusiasm for individual academic pursuits—not leading others, but not detracting either.	Demonstrates adequate teamwork, and willingness to work with others; rarely, if ever, demonstrates the ability to organize and lead group toward stated goals, assumes adequate responsibility for group tasks—not leading others, but not detracting either.
Detractor (1): Doesn't meet the standards personally, and detracts from others meeting the standards.	Does not arrive on time with materials; is not personally functioning at an adequate level, and detracts from the class's ability to function adequately.	Does not demonstrate organization and time management; poor-to-incompetent note-taking, word-processing, reading and writing skills—detracts from the class's ability to function adequately.	Demonstrates little or no mastery of course requirements and no facility or flexibility in using expected learner outcomes—detracts from the class's ability to function adequately.	Demonstrates little if any persistence, dedication, curiosity, or enthusiasm for individual academic pursuits—detracts from the class's ability to function adequately.	Demonstrates poor teamwork and an inability to work with others; demonstrates an inability to organize and lead group toward stated goals, assumes no responsibility for group tasks, and detracts from the class's ability to function adequately.
Note: An individual who is progressing toward a higher rating (e.g. a 3 or a 5), but who has not fully arrived (i.e., demonstrates some but not all of the criteria, or demonstrates criteria inconsistently) can be identified as a 2 or a 4.					

PERFORMANCE CHARACTER

HIGH/LEADER:

- I strive for excellence and I am motivated to give my best effort.
- I approach learning as a lifelong process.
- I view difficulties as opportunities to strengthen my understanding.
- I strive to acquire the knowledge that characterizes an educated person.
- I possess healthy self-confidence and a positive attitude.
- I work well with others.
- I know standards of quality and I am committed to high-quality work and I take pride in my work.
- I take responsibility for my mistakes.
- I contribute to family, classroom, and community.
- I formulate life goals and ways to pursue them.
- I am a good example and a positive influence.
- I practice to improve the skills and habits required for excellence.

SUFFICIENT/PARTICIPANT:

- I carry out responsibilities but do not take a leadership role.
- I demonstrate adequate organization and time management.
- I demonstrate adequate persistence, curiosity, and dedication but lack intensity and consistency.
- I demonstrate adequate mastery of course requirements.

INEFFECTIVE/DETRACTOR:

- I demonstrate little or no mastery of course requirement .
- I am unorganized and manage my time poorly.
- I demonstrate little persistence, dedication, or enthusiasm for academic pursuits.
- I demonstrate poor teamwork and assume no responsibility for group tasks.
- I put forth little effort on tasks.
- I detract others from their work and create chaos and anarchy.
- I am defiant at times.

MORAL CHARACTER

HIGH/LEADER:

- I possess good judgment, moral reasoning, and ethical wisdom.
- I treat others with respect and care.
- I make responsible personal choices that contribute to continuous self-development, a healthy lifestyle, and a positive future.
- I am a good example and a positive influence.
- I use ethical means to achieve my performance goals.
- I take responsibility to do what's right.
- I take a stand for what is right and assume leadership for influencing others to do what is right.

SUFFICIENT/PARTICIPANT:

- I do the right thing when someone is watching.
- I do not always use ethical means to achieve my performance goals.
- I do not possess good judgment consistently.
- I show little respect and care for others.
- A healthy lifestyle and a positive future are not a priority for me.
- I give in to peer pressure.

INEFFECTIVE/DETRACTOR:

- I do not respect or care about others.
- I lack self-control and make very poor moral decisions.
- I cheat.
- I lie.
- I steal.
- I do not care about doing what's right.

(School) SELF-REFLECTION

I WILL FOLLOW THE VIRTUES OF OUR SCHOOL TOUCHSTONE.
I WILL GIVE MY PERSONAL BEST.
I WILL DO THE RIGHT THING BECAUSE IT IS THE RIGHT THING TO DO!

Please rate yourself this nine weeks with a: 4 , 3, 2, 1, or 0.
4 = 100% / Your personal best and 0 = 0% / No / Never / There was no effort on my part at all.

Nine weeks:	**1st**	**2nd**	**3rd**	**4th**
RESPONSIBILITY:				
• I brought needed supplies to class.	____	____	____	____
• I completed assignments, always giving my personal best!	____	____	____	____
• I completed my assignments in a timely manner.	____	____	____	____
• I had excellent class attendance.	____	____	____	____
• I participated in class.	____	____	____	____
• I persisted until I met the (school) high expectations.	____	____	____	____
RESPECT:				
• I followed the rules and expected procedures.	____	____	____	____
• I worked cooperatively.	____	____	____	____
• I respected other people.	____	____	____	____
• I respected other peoples' property.	____	____	____	____
• I respected myself.	____	____	____	____
• I was polite and mannerly.	____	____	____	____
HONESTY:				
• I did my own work and did not copy from another student.	____	____	____	____
• I told the truth even when it was very difficult.	____	____	____	____
CARE:				
• I was friendly and kind to others.	____	____	____	____
• I helped others.	____	____	____	____
• I listened to others.	____	____	____	____
PERSONAL BEST EFFORT:				
• I worked on a task until it was completed.	____	____	____	____
• I met or exceeded the objectives of the task or lesson.	____	____	____	____
• I viewed difficulties as opportunities to strengthen my understanding.	____	____	____	____
• I put forth the time needed for the task or assignment.	____	____	____	____
• I prepared for a lesson or assessment by doing my homework.	____	____	____	____
• I requested help as needed.	____	____	____	____
• I studied.	____	____	____	____

FIRST NINE WEEK GOAL: ________________________________

SECOND NINE WEEK GOAL________________________________

THIRD NINE WEEK GOAL:________________________________

FOURTH NINE WEEK GOAL:________________________________

FIRST 9 WEEKS

(School) SELF-REFLECTION

I WILL FOLLOW THE VIRTUES OF OUR SCHOOL TOUCHSTONE.
I WILL GIVE MY PERSONAL BEST.
I WILL DO THE RIGHT THING BECAUSE IT IS THE RIGHT THING TO DO!

☺ =YES! BEST! 😐 =OK, I CAN DO BETTER. ☹ =NO! HELP!

RESPONSIBILITY:

I brought needed supplies to class.	☺	😐	☹
I turned in my work on time.	☺	😐	☹
I came to school every day.	☺	😐	☹
I participated in class.	☺	😐	☹

RESPECT:

I followed the rules.	☺	😐	☹
I was polite.	☺	😐	☹
I listened.	☺	😐	☹

HONESTY:

I did my own work.	☺	😐	☹
I told the truth.	☺	😐	☹

CARE:

I was friendly and kind to others.	☺	😐	☹

PERSONAL BEST EFFORT:

I worked hard.	☺	😐	☹
I asked for help as needed.	☺	😐	☹
I studied.	☺	😐	☹
I did my homework.	☺	😐	☹
I always try to do my personal best!	☺	😐	☹
I like school.	☺	😐	☹

My strengths: ____

____

____

Steps I will take to improve: ____

____

____

Effort rubrics

For classroom use, an effort rubric is helpful to use with assignments or class projects. If used regularly, students get into the habit of reflecting on how much effort they put into a task. Self-awareness is the first step to correcting a deficiency. The following rubric was adapted from the *Smart & Good* book (also from the work of Marzano[26]) and includes both effort and achievement. Like the previous rubrics, the scale not only leads to self-assessment, but also defines what "effort" entails.

Name ______________________________ Grade Level __________

Directions: Rate yourself from 1 to 4 on the effort that you put into a task and how it related to your achievement.

Effort Rubric. My effort was a _____

1 = I put very little effort into the task.
2 = I put some effort into the task but stopped working when difficulties arose.
3 = I worked hard on the task until it was completed. I pushed myself to work on the task even when difficulties arose and a solution was not immediately apparent.
4 = I worked on the task until it was completed. I pushed myself to work on the task even when difficulties arose and a solution was not immediately apparent. I viewed difficulties as opportunities to strengthen my understanding.

Achievement Rubric. My achievement was a _____

1 = I did not meet the objectives of this lesson.
2 = I met a few of the objectives of the task or lesson, but I did not meet others.
3 = I met the objectives of the task or lesson.
4 = I exceeded the objectives of the task or lesson.

There are many other rubrics that can be adopted for classroom use; our schools adopted many from Marzano's *Classroom Instruction that Works* or *A Handbook For Classroom Instruction That Works*. We recommend consulting his work for additional information and rubric formats.

Choosing the right rubric depends on the age and performance level of your students. Younger and less motivated students will need more information about what effort looks like and perhaps an external motivation to complete the rubric. Some schools and teachers give "points" towards grades for completing the rubrics; others don't need to do this. While the goal is to get students to take responsibility for their own learning and rely on internal rewards, most students (and adults for that matter!) need some external motivation to develop a new habit.

Modeling

Modeling appropriate behavior would appear to be the easiest component in developing student character, yet it is the most difficult. Most teachers believe they are ethical people and that they are setting a good example for youth in the classroom. But effective modeling is much more than the absence of unethical or illegal behaviors. Modeling requires deliberate and intentional action and a great deal of self-reflection and honesty on the part of the teacher. The teacher reflection piece on page 41 is a useful tool for teachers to use as a self-check on whether they are modeling high performance and moral character.

"Everyone thinks of changing the world, but no one thinks of changing himself."

Leo Tolstoy

One of the most important aspects of modeling for educators is to make sure they hold themselves to the same standards they ask of students—treating others with respect, coming prepared to class and doing their best work. We have to be willing to take a critical, honest look at what we are modeling in the classroom. That is why having another teacher or instructional coach observe and make suggestions is so helpful. For example, one teacher asked for help in getting students to come to class on time. The character coach arranged to come into the classroom to observe the teacher and make suggestions. She arrived in the classroom just as the bell was sounding, but the teacher wasn't there. She asked the students if they knew where the teacher was, and was told, "She's always late."

"I have come to a frightening conclusion. I am the decisive element in the classroom. It is my personal approach that creates the climate. It is my daily mood that makes the weather. As a teacher, I possess tremendous power to make a child's life miserable or joyous. I can be a tool of torture or an instrument of inspiration. I can humiliate or humor, hurt or heal. In all situations it is my response that decides whether a crisis will be escalated or de-escalated, a child humanized or dehumanized."

Dr. Haim Ginott, *Teacher and Child*

One of the most impactful resources we used was the work of Dr. Hal Urban. All of the schools received multiple copies of his book *Lessons from the Classroom*[27] and were encouraged to use it as a book study or in their PLC's. Dr. Urban also presented workshops for both the group of all schools, and also at several individual schools. Dr. Urban, a 30-year veteran teacher, emphasizes modeling and relationships in the classroom, and provides a rich resource of classroom management techniques, ways to build positive relationships, and how these can boost learning.

One of Hal Urban's lessons is the power of language. The words teachers and students use in classrooms have the power to destroy a student's self-worth or restore their confidence. Building relationships begins with how we treat others, what we say and how we say it. Dr. Urban provides two lists—the "Dirty Thirty" and the "Thoughtful Thirty." He compiled these lists over years of teaching and asking students and others "What kind of language drags you down? What are some of the things you don't like to hear other people talk about?" The "Dirty Thirty" list made him realize how many toxic words are used in classrooms—including his own! Compiling the list helped him make a conscious effort to eliminate as many of them as he could.

THE DIRTY THIRTY

1. Bragging
2. Swearing and other gross-out language
3. Gossip
4. Angry words
5. Lies
6. Mean-spirited and hurtful words
7. Judging others
8. Playing "poor me"—the self-pity game
9. Making discouraging remarks
10. Embarrassing and humiliating people
11. Excessive faultfinding and criticism
12. Complaining, moaning, whining
13. Rude and inconsiderate language
14. Teasing
15. Manipulation
16. Trying to impress others with phony and insincere comments
17. Ethnic and racial slurs
18. Sexist comments
19. Age-related put-downs
20. Being negative—always pointing out what's wrong
21. Threats
22. Arguing
23. Interrupting—not letting the other person finish
24. Playing "trump"—always topping someone else's story
25. Being a know-it-all
26. False flattery
27. Yelling
28. Talking down to people—being condescending
29. Exaggerating
30. Blaming and accusing others

THE THOUGHTFUL THIRTY

1. Give encouragement
2. Express thanks
3. Acknowledge others
4. Extend greetings
5. Give a compliment
6. Congratulate someone
7. Teach, give instructions
8. Offer words of comfort
9. Inspire others
10. Celebrate and cheer
11. Inquire, express interest
12. Mend relationships
13. Make others laugh
14. Show faith and trust
15. Share good news
16. Praise, honor, build up
17. Express caring
18. Show understanding and empathy
19. Give approval
20. Extend an invitation
21. Show courtesy and respect
22. Give advice and counsel
23. Apologize
24. Forgive
25. Offer to help
26. Tell the truth
27. Point out the good
28. Use terms of affection
29. Provide valuable information
30. Communicate love

From Urban, H. (2008). *Lessons from the classroom*, pages 78-79, 92

After identifying the words that hurt or made people feel bad, Hal Urban began asking people, "What words and actions make other people and ourselves feel good?" This led to the "Thoughtful Thirty" and his intentional efforts to model these types of communications in his classroom and with colleagues. The box above includes Dr. Urban's lists.

First week of school plans

> "What we do the first two weeks of school will determine our success or failure for the rest of the school year. We will either win or lose our class on the first days of school."
>
> **Harry & Rosemary Wong**

Most teachers know that the beginning of the school year sets the tone for the rest of the year. Many have read the books by Harry and Rosemary Wong[28] on the subject. During our second year of implementation, we asked all staff to create a plan for the first week of school that featured the development of performance and moral character, and that utilized some of the classroom strategy resources (Hal Urban, Kagan, rubrics, etc.) they had been provided.

One of our schools chose to distribute the following letter and list of "what makes a good teacher" to each staff member at the end of the school year that described principles of good teaching (taken from both Urban's and Wong's books) and asked each staff member to create meaningful lessons for the first week of school. It was strongly suggested that giving up some academic time early in the year would positively influence the learning environment throughout the year because students would behave better, work harder, and perform at a higher academic level.

Kids don't care how much we know until they know how much we care.

Dear (school name) Staff,

Academic performance is enhanced when the culture within a school is one of mutual respect, responsibility, cleanliness, and hard work. The motto of our character education initiative is "We take education seriously, we honor the rules, and we help each other succeed."

With this in mind, please develop your plan for the first week of school next year. Use the attached list of qualities of good teaching, based on the work of Harry and Rosemary Wong and Hal Urban, to help guide your planning.

A Number One goal for the year is to create, with students' help, the best possible environment in our classrooms, a place where everyone feels welcome and confident that their classmates and the teacher will treat them with respect.

Sincerely,
(Principal)

What Makes a Good Teacher?

Good teachers...

...create a caring community. Students are more likely to accept the values and rules of the group when they feel accepted and affirmed by the group. Peer culture is a powerful influence so we need to help shape a positive peer culture. When students are part of a legitimate caring moral community, they learn morality by living it. Through daily experiences, respect and care gradually become habits—part of their character. It is our "personal" approach (how we treat our students) that creates the climate.

...protect the atmosphere from toxic words. We underestimate the power of words! We will discuss the things people say that poison the atmosphere—the types of things we don't like to hear. We will discuss swearing and other offensive words. We will emphasize courtesy and a professional level of language.

...nourish the atmosphere with kind and affirming words. We will teach kids to build up instead of tear down. We will look for the good, find the good, and celebrate the good.

...start every class with something positive. "Does anyone have some good news to share today?" or "Who or what are you thankful for?" or "Who has a kind word?"

...and their students, have a mission and set goals. We will consider writing a personal and class mission statement. Motivation comes from within. We will not try to motivate—we will try to inspire!

...use the power of visible reminders. Putting all of our posters up before students arrive adds color but no meaning. We will discuss and post each visible reminder.

...help their students both own and honor the rules.

...set high standards and have high expectations. We will consider putting our policies in writing. We will ask students what are their expectations of us.

...help their students discover the power of choice. We will discuss the greatest power that students will ever have—the power to choose.

...tell good stories. Most kids will tune out a lecture but all kids will listen to a good story.

...use the power of quotations. Wise sayings help us make our point.

...laugh with their students.

...catch kids doing things right. We will let the student and the parents know.

...form partnerships with parents.

...start teaching at the door. They individually greet and welcome each student into the classroom. It is one of the simplest, least time consuming, enjoyable, and energizing thing we can do as a teacher. Students may need to be taught the social skills of eye contact, a firm handshake, and a smile.

...post the assignment on the board. "Class Ready" Students begin the assignment as soon as they enter the room, then take roll.

...rehearse/reinforce procedures.

...teach manners and the Golden Rule. Not all students have learned common courtesy. "What we accept, we teach. What we permit, we promote." We deal with infractions as soon as they occur, without losing our composure or yelling. We will not make the student look bad in the presence of classmates. Students need to know early on that we're in charge, they need to know what our standards and expectations are, and they need to know what will not be tolerated. Everyone operates more effectively when their boundaries are clearly defined.

...are proactive, not reactive. Frequent rude eruptions waste class time. We will not wait until a student does something wrong and then "react" to it. We will take a proactive approach.

Teachers then created their personal plan for the first week of school on the form below. The form had to be signed by the teacher and principal, and most important to this process, was the follow up by the principal the following year. The following is an example of a plan that was created using this format by a middle school teacher.

MY PERSONAL PLAN FOR THE FIRST WEEK OF SCHOOL

I will

- Teach manners by example and discussions/activities.
- Greet every student, every day, every class.
- Display the Golden Rule bulletin board.
- Discuss that subs are "guest teachers" and how they should be treated.
- Send home parent letter.
- Create rules/expectations (students and mine) with each class.
- Set first 9 weeks goals—academic and personal.
- Teach study skills and organization skills.
- Find out student expectations of me and the class.
- Find out how my students want my room to look, feel, sound.
- Discuss location of posted homework and being "class-ready."
- Student surveys of school strengths/weaknesses.
- Have an "issue" box that will allow students to anonymously jot down any concerns or questions. Once a week, address some of these issues.
- Discuss and acknowledge student achievement whether it be passing a book quiz, reaching a success zone, improving in test scores, etc.
- Work on supporting each other through both success and failure.

Day 1: Post each of the 4 elements on a separate piece of poster paper. Initiate discussion. Encourage description of what this element would look like.

Day 2: Using the 4 element posters for a "carousel" activity, students will be divided into 4 groups and rotate, adding written phrases and comments relative to each element. Each group will report out on the last poster in their rotation.

Day 3: As a class, develop rules for the classroom.

Day 4: As your teacher, what do you want me to promise you? (Journal Response)

Day 5: What can I challenge you to give me in return? (Journal Response and oral discussion)

My plan addresses the following:

- **A secure class environment**
- **The promotion of fairness, equity, caring, and respect**
- **The contribution of students in meaningful ways**
- **The promotion of a caring school community and positive social relationships**

Teacher's Name:____________________ Principal's Signature:____________________

Classroom management to promote performance and moral character

One area that many teachers struggle with is classroom management. Most teachers will tell you that they received little preparation for this in their undergraduate training. The goal is to create a physically and emotionally safe and secure classroom of mutual respect, fairness and caring, where students are responsible and contribute in meaningful ways. Too often though, teachers are reactive, not proactive when it comes to successfully managing a classroom. Because classroom management is tightly tied to how we deliver instruction and the time that is available for learning, lessons that engage and motivate students minimize management concerns.

Many teachers are reluctant to change how they are teaching, especially if they are for the most part successful in managing their classrooms. However, over time, we did find many staff had a "thirst" for time to share with and observe other teachers, and many were eager to have a coach observe them and offer suggestions for how to more effectively engage students.

Some of our project schools identified discipline as a significant problem in their school and teachers requested help with classroom management to help reduce classroom discipline issues. There are many excellent resources on effective classroom management. We found the following strategies, some of which have already been discussed, as effective in promoting performance and moral character:

1. **Leader to detractor scale.** This rubric (see page 75) was very helpful for both middle and high school teachers who were experiencing problems managing classroom behavior. It helped by establishing expectations for behavior and placing the responsibility for assessing behavior on the student. It also defines for the student what behavior is associated with being a leader.
2. **Personal greeting of students at the door.** Also discussed above (page 64), the simple act of greeting students each day at the classroom door was a powerful way to establish a respectful relationship with students. Mutual respect is critical to classroom management.
3. **Student participation in forming classroom rules.** In his book, *Lessons from the Classroom*, Hal Urban also discusses his strategies for establishing classroom rules. His view is that students must participate in establishing classroom rules, rather than having them imposed by the teacher. Aren't we more likely to follow rules that we helped write and voted on than ones given to us? Urban has further noted that students sometimes suggest more stringent rules than he would select. We provide examples below (see page 91) on how he accomplished this.

4. **Consistent enforcement of classroom rules.** Dr. Urban also stresses that once the class has written and voted on the rules, the teacher must be consistent in enforcing them. If students see that the teacher only selectively enforces, they won't abide by them. Some of our teachers found this very difficult to put into practice. In one classroom we observed, the teacher had some of Hal Urban's "positive words" posted around the classroom and made a point of showing them to us, along with the classroom rules his class had selected. One of the rules was no sleeping in class, yet we saw several students with their heads down on the desk, not participating in the classroom discussion. The teacher was also having difficulty managing the discussion because he was allowing a lot of behavior that was clearly in violation of the class rules.

"What we permit, we promote."

Hal Urban

5. **Lessons that actively involve students.** Student engagement, discussed in more detail below, places more of the responsibility for learning on students. When students are actively engaged in classroom activities, there is less time for inappropriate behavior.

6. **Clear behavioral classroom expectations.** Resources such as the Leader to Detractor rubric (above) and Positive Behavior Supports (PBS) define in behavioral terms what is expected. The more specific expected behavior is spelled out, the more information students have. If they don't know what is expected, they can't comply.

7. **Teacher modeling of expected behaviors.** Discussed many times above, teachers must model behaviors they expect of their students. Middle and high school students are keenly tuned in to what they perceive as "hypocrisy" on the part of adults—"They want us to turn our papers in on time, but they take forever to grade them."

8. **Positive relationships with students.** Chapter 5 provides numerous strategies for establishing relationships with students. Students are less likely to misbehave if they like and respect the teacher. We don't want to disappoint people who care about us.

9. **Classroom climate of mutual respect.** Positive relationships among the students in the class help establish trust and a feeling of safety and cooperation. Hal Urban's book, *Lessons from the Classroom* also provides multiple examples of strategies to promote a respectful classroom climate.

We also provided the following general guidelines for classroom management during our teacher workshops:

- **Be Proactive, Not Reactive.** Careful planning is key!
- **Expect the Best.** Label students with positive qualities while telling them how you expect them to act.
- **Understand the Symptoms of Misbehavior.** Students will do many things to get attention, even if it is negative attention. Some students want to control the situation because they have no control over anything outside of school life. Some students are bored or unchallenged. Some are masking feelings of inadequacy or failure.
- **Create a comfortable and natural environment.** Be mindful of the room arrangement, a comfortable classroom will enable students to feel safe and secure, reduce the number of distractions, provide a smooth flow of students, and support more time on task and allow for all students to have access to the teacher.
- **Humor.** Buy a joke book and start your class each day with a joke of the day. Use cartoons to accompany the content that you are teaching. Use a warm-up activity with a riddle on the board to be answered individually or in teams or partners to grab the attention of the class. Invite students to bring in jokes and cartoons related to class topics (a great opportunity as to what jokes are appropriate and which are not!)
- **Hook them in.** The brain likes novelty because whatever the brain perceives as unusual wakes it up and causes it to produce norepinephrine. You have to capture students' attention before you can maintain it. This can be accomplished by varying the way you deliver instruction, rearranging the seating arrangement, relating lessons to the "real world," showing the relevance of lessons, or animating a lesson with emotion or drama. Students will pick up on a teacher's boredom with teaching or the subject; it takes effort to make subjects come alive or be relevant.
- **Communicate effectively.** Good communicators maintain eye contact, use "I" rather than "you" messages, de-emphasize the negative, and use consistent, calm, low-profile (low volume) interventions.
- **Separate the disciplinary infraction from the student.** Maintain respect while informing the student that you will not tolerate this type of behavior. Communicate acceptance, caring, and respect for every student.

Student engagement and student voice

Student engagement occurs when students make a psychological investment in learning. Students take pride not simply in earning the formal indicators of success (grades), but in understanding the material and incorporating or internalizing it in their lives. To really understand the importance of student engagement, teachers must first realize it is the teacher's primary responsibility to engage the students, as opposed to the teacher expecting students to come to class naturally and automatically engaged. Students also do not become engaged unless they feel some connection to the school, so relationship building is the first step in engaging students in learning.[30]

Create an Emotionally Safe Classroom

"Students who have been shamed or belittled by the teacher or another student will not effectively engage in challenging tasks. Consider having a rule such as "We do not put others down, tell others to shut up, or laugh at people." Apply it to yourself as well as your students. This is the foundation of a supportive, collaborative learning environment. To learn and grow, one must take risks, but most people will not take risks in an emotionally unsafe environment."

Tristan de Frondeville

Student voice requires including the perspectives and influences of students in the classroom learning environment, projects, procedures, policies, and programs. Student voice is a way to involve students in the organizational structure of the school and engaging them in the school community. Common examples of incorporating student voice are: student leadership groups, student councils, and student focus/action groups. However, to be effective, efforts to include student voice must involve all students and student populations—specifically giving those students who are typically not involved an opportunity to share their voices and participate. Allowing student voice also institutes a framework for developing and implementing student-directed projects.

"Create a school platform that shouts: This is your education. Speak up and get involved!"

Adapted from Ontario Ministry of Education

In schools where student voice is valued and promoted, students are more engaged in the learning process. Student voice places the responsibility for learning with the student. Students learn that they have the opportunity to take control of their learning by becoming more engaged.

Our project placed a major emphasis on engaging students and encouraging student voice. Multiple resources were provided as well as professional development. Some teachers adapted and created additional materials. We share the most successful below.

Reflection

One school developed a teacher reflection tool so that teachers would become more intentional in promoting student voice and engagement. They also regularly shared strategies revealed by using this tool.

Reflecting on My Current Practices

1. How do I engage students in the classroom?
2. What are the challenges I face with engaging students?
3. In what ways am I proactive?
4. What questioning techniques do I use to involve all students?
5. How do I show I effectively listen to students?
6. What is the most effective strategy I use in the classroom that I would be willing to share?

Another teacher developed reflection tools for students to encourage them to reflect on their own learning, encourage personal responsibility, and provide (anonymous) feedback to teachers on how good a job they are doing. The boxes below are two tools for students, which not only help students self-reflect, but also empowers them and conveys that the teacher values their input.

Discussion Questions/Prompts as the Semester comes to a close:

1. Are you generally satisfied with the first semester this year?
2. Have you accomplished as much and done as well as expected?
3. Are there any obstacles that you feel interfered with your personal growth? If so, what are they? What do you feel you can do to overcome these obstacles?
4. Who, or what, has had the greatest influence in helping you thus far this year?
5. If there is one thing you could subtract or erase from your first semester, what would it be?
6. What is the most valuable lesson or piece of wisdom that you feel you have learned in life in thus far?
7. How can you apply that wisdom to your next semester?

Grading the Teacher

1. Please write in this space the things I do well as a teacher:

2. Please write in this space the ways in which I could improve:

3. What grade would you give me at this point? ______

Classroom rules

We included in the classroom management section above Hal Urban's advice, "What you permit, you promote." Teachers often deal with disruptive behavior by ignoring it, which usually backfires because the behaviors escalate. This continues until the teacher loses his or her temper and starts yelling. Urban details how each year he led students through activities that guided them in creating the classroom rules. By giving them a voice in choosing these guidelines, students had more of a "stake" in abiding by them.

Several schools found Hal Urban's tools on the power of words and language and creating classroom rules to be particularly useful. An affirmation assignment was shown on page 54, and we have included his tool for making classroom rules below.

If We Made the Rules

Students would not be allowed to...	Students would be encouraged to...
1. ______	1. ______
2. ______	2. ______
3. ______	3. ______
4. ______	4. ______
5. ______	5. ______

From Hal Urban, *Lessons from the Classroom*

Instructional strategies

Dr. Spencer Kagan is an internationally acclaimed researcher, presenter and author. Kagan strategies are used with great success in many classrooms, elementary through college. Kagan calls his approach to character education a "structural approach," and his emphasis is that students learn character by the way they are taught, rather than through direct instruction (which he calls the "curriculum" approach.) We included a number of his strategies in our professional development workshops, examples of which follow.

Kagan argues that it is inefficient to teach lessons on traits such as respect, for two reasons. One, for learning to "stick," it must be repeated and reviewed periodically. With the amount of curriculum that teachers now need to teach, they don't have time to teach and re-teach lessons specifically on each desired virtue. "A lecture on helpfulness does not promote helpfulness nearly as much as the experience of peer tutoring. *How* we teach forms character more than *what* we teach. There is a curriculum embedded in instruction, and *it is the embedded curriculum that determines character formation more than the explicit curriculum*."[31] Second, by embedding the learning of the character structures in how curriculum is taught, there is better transference to actual practice. So, as in the above example, rather than learning about helpfulness, the students actually practice being helpful by peer tutoring. Another example is the Kagan structure, "Paraphrase Passport." "Students may be asked to use *Paraphrase Passport* while discussing a controversial topic. The passport to speak is to accurately paraphrase the person who spoke right before you. Because of this structure, students learn to listen to and respect points of view different from their own. In this approach, rather than being taught lessons about the importance of respect, students practice respect."[32] It is important however, when using Kagan structures, to reinforce the embedded trait you are trying to teach—use the language to label a student's behavior."Thank you for being respectful of Johnny and listening to what he has to say." For more information on Kagan's instructional methods, go to http://www.kaganonline.com.

Secondary literacy strategies to build performance and moral character

One of our ancillary project goals was to use secondary literacy strategies to promote the development of performance and moral character. Middle and high school educators immediately grasped the value of developing both literacy and character. During the second year of the project we created a "spa strategies newsletter" that was distributed monthly to everyone. We called them "spa strategies" because just like a spa, they were designed to rejuvenate—in this case, teaching. Each newsletter contained one secondary literacy strategy that promoted multiple performance and moral character values. For example, one strategy was the "Guided Lecture Procedure for Active Listening" (adapted from Vacca & Vacca[33]) which is a more structured way to present material to students in a lecture format. It also teaches self-discipline, diligence, cooperation and self-assessment. The complete set of newsletters is available on the web at http://www.charactereducationohio.org/programs/creating-smart-and-good-schools-project/newsletter-archive/.

Classroom grading systems

As we have discussed earlier, some staff will not think character education pertains to their classroom. In one of the high schools there was an Algebra teacher who did not see the connection. However, when she learned more about performance character, she quickly began reflecting and redesigning her teaching strategies and policies. The biggest change was her decision to not count homework in the student's grade. She had been frustrated for years that students would fail the tests but be able to pass the course because of homework grades. She knew the students hadn't learned the material and would be handicapped in future mathematics coursework. Although she knew it would be unpopular, she took the "plunge" and changed her classroom grading so that grades were based on tests, quizzes and projects. Her greatest fear was that too many students would fail, and she would have students, parents and administrators pressuring her to change the grades. She was thrilled though, when at the end of the first year of implementation, student grades remained about the same. At first she was disheartened that the change hadn't made a difference, but then realized that grades now represented real learning and understanding of the course content, rather than homework completion. The students had "stepped

Performance Enhancement in Mathematics

Do you want to be successful in Algebra II? What does this quote have to do with your success in Algebra II? How does this quote affect life outside of the mathematics classroom? Please write your reflections in the space below.

Quote of the Day

"Everything can be taken from us except one thing—the freedom to choose our attitude in any set of circumstances."

Victor Frankl

up" to her challenge, worked harder and been successful. But, it wasn't just a matter of changing the grading system. The teacher developed a system of supports and reflection tools to help students along the way.

To begin the year, she wrote a letter to her students and their parents to explain the new grading policy, give a rationale, explain procedures, and student responsibilities. It also required both the student and parent to sign and return the form. It is a well-constructed letter that, because of its length, is included in the Appendix on pages 135-136. It should provide ideas on how to reach out to students and parents in an effort to give them a better understanding of class expectations and goal setting.

In the letter, the teacher conveyed that she still valued homework as necessary for students to learn the material, but it couldn't be used to "prop up" failing test grades. It also removed the incentive for students to copy each other's homework; a practice she feared was rewarded when students could earn points for homework. To support her change in classroom policies and to promote the development of the performance character traits she wanted her students to develop, this enthusiastic teacher used a "Quote of the Day." Each quote was on a full sheet of paper with the beginning of the task being the same for each one. The examples above are a few of the quotes she found related to performance character.

Performance Enhancement in Mathematics

Do you want to be successful in Algebra II? What does this quote have to do with your success in Algebra II? How does this quote affect life outside of the mathematics classroom? Please write your reflections in the space below.

Quote of the Day

"Discipline yourself and others won't have to."

John Wooden

As you see in the above examples, the task at the top of the paper is always the same. The quote is changed daily. Below are a few other quotes this performance character driven teacher used:

- Hold yourself to a higher standard than anybody expects of you. Never excuse yourself. (Henry Ward Beecher)
- The best preparation for tomorrow is to do today's work superbly well. (William Osler)
- There is no such thing as failure. There is only giving up too soon. (Jonas Salk)
- You must do the thing you think you cannot do. (Eleanor Roosevelt)
- Excellence is not an act, but a habit. We are what we repeatedly do. (Aristotle)
- A teacher opens the door, but you must enter yourself. (Chinese Proverb)

This teacher also developed reflection tools that she regularly had students use to self-assess their work ethic, shown below. Part one assesses performance character, part two assesses study skills and work ethic, and part three held students accountable for the classroom rules they had agreed upon.

Performance Enhancement in Mathematics: 10 Day Check-up/Tune-up

Part One

We have just completed ten days of examining ten words that should help enhance your performance in mathematics class. By each of ten words circle your level of use for that characteristic.

I.	Effort	Always	Usually	Sometimes	Rarely	Never
II.	Positive attitude	Always	Usually	Sometimes	Rarely	Never
III.	Perseverance	Always	Usually	Sometimes	Rarely	Never
IV.	Goal setting	Always	Usually	Sometimes	Rarely	Never
V.	Progress monitoring	Always	Usually	Sometimes	Rarely	Never
VI.	Self-discipline	Always	Usually	Sometimes	Rarely	Never
VII.	Diligence	Always	Usually	Sometimes	Rarely	Never
VIII.	Orderliness	Always	Usually	Sometimes	Rarely	Never
IX.	Responsibility	Always	Usually	Sometimes	Rarely	Never
X.	Strong work ethic	Always	Usually	Sometimes	Rarely	Never

Part Two

Do you have your notebook with all your work set up and with you in class every day?

Have you completed all homework?

Are you up to date in completion of your Notetaking Guide?

Do you ask for help when you don't understand an assignment?

Part Three

The class wrote a list of rules to follow. *Check off* all the rules that you consistently follow every day in class.

1. _____ Do your own work
2. _____ Pay attention
3. _____ No distractions
4. _____ Follow the Golden Rule
5. _____ Use manners
6. _____ Show respect for others and their property
7. _____ Follow directions
8. _____ Participate
9. _____ Be considerate of students that do not understand the lesson

She also created questionnaires to make sure students were keeping up with their work as well as encouraging them to self-reflect on their work ethic and performance, and relating it to their performance on tests. Below is an example of one of the tools she developed.

1. Did you read Chapter ______?	Yes	No	Parts
2. Did you fill out the Notetaking Guide for Chapter ______?	Yes	No	Parts
3. Did you complete all homework assignments for Chapter ______?	Yes	No	Parts

4. When you cannot work a problem or do a homework assignment do you: (Circle all that apply.)

- Phone a friend
- Ask questions in class
- Come before school for additional help
- Come after school for additional help
- Go to after school tutoring on Tuesdays or Thursdays
- Form a study group
- Google the topic
- Seek another teacher to explain the topic
- All of the above
- None of the above

Other____

5. How does your test grade compare with what you thought it should be?

6. How does your test grade compare with your effort (see 1-4 above)?

7. What would help you improve your grade in this class?

8. When you are absent how do you go about catching up with the class?

9. Explain how you prepared for this test.

This particular teacher really understood the importance of checking in with the students throughout the semester and worked to catch them before they fell too far behind. The following is another example of how she got the students to self-reflect on their performance. By frequently using these self-assessments, she was able to identify students who needed help. The list of questions also gave students a list of strategies they could use to improve their performance.

Did you do the review assignment?	Yes	No
Do you do your homework on a daily basis?	Yes	No
Did you read the covered sections in the book and look at the examples?	Yes	No
Did you go over the mid-chapter test?	Yes	No
Did you review your notes?	Yes	No
Did you ask questions before the test?	Yes	No
Did you ask questions daily about homework?	Yes	No
If you miss a question on a test, quiz, or homework, do you work until you understand the reason you made a mistake?	Yes	No
Do you work with a tutor?	Yes	No
Did you ask for extra help after/before school?	Yes	No
Do you do the extra problems offered in the back of the book?	Yes	No
Do you do the practice test in the back of the book?	Yes	No
Do you believe that you can do the math problems?	Yes	No

Comments:

What else can the teacher do to help?

Notes

25. See R. Berger. (2003). *An Ethic of Excellence*. Portsmouth, NH: Heinemann, for an interesting discussion of how to help students understand and produce quality work.
26. See Lickona & Davidson (2005), pg 109, original source R. Marzano, D. Pickering, & J.E. Pollock. Classroom instruction that works: Research-based strategies for increasing student achievement. (Alexandria, VA: Association for Supervision & Curriculum Development, 2001).
27. Urban, H. (2008). *w*. Great Lessons Press.
28. Wong, H. K. & Wong, R. T. (2009). *The First days of school*. Mountainview, CA: Harry K. Wong Publications.
29. Sprenger, M. (2005). *How to teach so students remember*. Alexandria, VA: Association for Supervision and Curriculum Development.
30. DeFrondeville, T. (2012) Ten steps to better student engagement. *Edutopia*, retrieved February 2012 at http://www.edutopia.org/project-learning-teaching-strategies
31. Kagan, S. (2002). The structural approach to character education. The 4th & 5th Rs Respect and responsibility. 8 (3), 1-3.
32. Kagan, S. (2002). The structural approach to character education. The 4th & 5th Rs Respect and responsibility. 8 (3), 1-3.
33. Vacca, R. T. & Vacca, J. L. (1989). Content Area Reading. New York: Harper Collins Publishing.

9

Youth Leadership

We include a separate chapter on youth leadership because all of our project schools implemented some type of strategy to develop youth leadership. Students need to learn leadership skills in order to be successful, whether they go to college or directly into the workforce. Leadership, like student voice and engagement, empowers students and strengthens the connection to the school and community.

All schools utilized the following qualities and skills principles to plan their leadership activities.

QUALITIES OF A LEADER

Leaders generally possess a certain set of characteristics that enables them to be more effective. Leaders are often born with these qualities and they become part of the leader's personality. These are the "intangibles" that make leading appear easier.

CONFIDENCE

Leaders typically emote confidence. A strong belief in yourself makes it easier for others to believe in you.

COMMITMENT

No one can make a true impact by only giving a little bit. Commitment of time, energy and self is necessary for long term positive change.

POSITIVE OUTLOOK

Before one can make a difficult situation better, he/she must first believe that the situation can be improved. Sometimes it is difficult to see positives in the negative world, but not for a leader.

TRUST IN PEOPLE

No one person can do it all. A leader must have faith in others and trust that they are capable.

CHARISMA

This special magnetic appeal is what draws people to a leader.

EMPATHY

This ability that allows us to feel what others feel is the most important quality a leader has.

SKILLS OF A LEADER

Not everyone is born with the aforementioned leadership qualities. This does not however preclude them from becoming a leader. The following list is a list of skills that can be developed to help anyone improve their ability to lead.

LISTENING: To lead people you have to know their wants and needs. To know their wants and needs, you have to listen.

PERSONAL ORGANIZATION: Being organized helps reduce the stress of leading. Before you can organize others, you must be organized yourself.

DIPLOMACY: A leader can deal with stressful situations without arousing tension. They also have the ability to defuse problems with others.

GOAL SETTING: A leader must set clear goals before taking action. Goals provide direction and a sense of accomplishment.

RECRUITMENT: There is strength in numbers. Leaders can attract others, especially those that can help with the cause.

Individuals can work to improve these skills and provide an opportunity to be a more effective leader.

Student council

Participating in student council is one of the oldest, simplest ways to promote student leadership skills. However, it does not engage all students and thus, it is a good, but not sufficient strategy by itself. It needs to be one of a variety of leadership opportunities offered to students. One of the project schools had discontinued student council because the faculty sponsor retired. The school chose to re-instate it as part of the project, and took the opportunity to make the process more intentional and deliberate in developing leadership and character. Students who were interested in participating were asked to complete an extensive application that demonstrated their commitment to serving on student council and detailed their responsibilities. An abbreviated form of the application is included on pages 102-103.

Character Kids

One middle school sought to develop leadership skills with a group they called Character Kids. Participating students were role models for the student body. Each Character Kid had character-building responsibilities. Students had to apply to join and one student per homeroom was chosen each quarter, to maximize participation. Teachers were asked to encourage quieter students to apply, or those who were often overlooked or not involved in other activities. The application is on page 105. Like the student council application above, the application requires the student to self-reflect and make a formal commitment to the responsibilities of the group.

The 27 *Character Kids* met during their study halls and were introduced to character development and the importance of their personal "modeling." They brainstormed, discussed, and chose their desired roles to accomplish this mission. Their goals were to be examples for others, to develop character, to get more students involved, and to "warm their school climate."

Character Kids participated in many activities. They each chose one or more activities that were their responsibility for that quarter. Among the projects were:

- **Birthday recognition**: Students were responsible for organizing a daily list and making certain that every student's birthday was announced.
- **Birthday trio:** Students went to homerooms and sang "Happy Birthday" and presented students having birthdays with a small gift from the staff.

Application for Student Council

Directions: Student Council is service-oriented and has many responsibilities, including organizing school dances, food drives, coat drives, Valentine's Day candy grams, Spirit Day and much more. In order to become a member of Student Council, the following packet must be completed and turned in on time. A Student Council member must show good character and be dedicated and prepared to do a lot of work efficiently and on time. Meetings will be held on a regular basis. All meetings are mandatory and essential to the productivity of the team. As a Student Council member, you will be required to show that you are a student who consistently exhibits honor, respect and responsibility. You must have strong leadership skills and be able to take direction well.

Student Council Responsibilities:

a. Must be academically eligible.
b. Must maintain a high standard of ethics and excellence with a positive attitude.
c. Must be prepared and on time for all meetings.
d. Must be willing to learn new things and have lots of fun!

By completing this application, you are showing interest in participating in the Student Council Elections.

Student's Name ____ Grade__________

Office sought: ___President (8th Grade Only) ___Vice President ___Treasurer

Each of your teachers must sign to recommend you for Student Council

Teacher Signature/Recommendation:

1st bell ____ ____________________

2nd bell ____ ____________________

3rd bell ____ ____________________

4th bell ____ ____________________

5th bell ____ ____________________

6th bell ____ ____________________

7th bell ____ ____________________

List all extra-curricular activities/clubs in which you participate:

Do you have any previous leadership experience? Yes ___ No___
If yes, please explain:

Tell why we should choose you to participate in Student Council:

Application for Student Council (continued)

To be completed by a parent/guardian: Tell why you believe your child has the leadership skills and character qualities needed to effectively serve his/her student body:

Check the words that best describe your personality:

___low-key/quiet	___outgoing/social	___organized	___humorous
___trustworthy	___self-disciplined	___responsible	___respectful
___motivated	___kind	___goal-oriented	___loyal

If I had three wishes, they would be:

Please Read Carefully!

By signing this form, I acknowledge that I must commit to being an active participant. If elected, I pledge to abide by all of the school's rules. I also pledge to represent the students of the school to the best of my ability. Furthermore, I understand that my failure to do my duties could result in my impeachment.

I understand that all parts of the application must be completed and turned in on time in order to be considered as a candidate.

I also understand that my duties and obligations to Student Council are NOT excused because I am involved in other activities, clubs, organizations, or athletic teams.

Student Signature______________________________________ Date ____________

Parent Signature_______________________________________ Date ____________

- **Calendars:** Students were responsible for posting all upcoming events.
- **Virtue of the week:** every week students posted a "virtue of the week" and each day a "quote of the day." They were also responsible for displaying the "Good Behavior coupons." Each Friday one coupon was given to a student to receive free admission to the school's activity night.
- **Live Announcements:** Students produced live audio and video announcements, created "commercials," shared daily current events, read the quote of the day and daily messages from Project Wisdom, and led the entire student body in reciting the school touchstone. Two students served as co-directors. A staff member met with them on a regular basis but the production was completely student led.
- **Student Ambassadors:** Two students from each grade level were chosen for this position. They "welcomed" new students to the school, introduced them to the staff, familiarized them with the building, and walked them through their schedule. One of the tech classes put together Welcome Kits which were customized school logo bags filled with small gifts and information.
- **Sunshine Club:** Students planned ways for the student body to recognize the "forgotten few": bus drivers, secretaries, cooks, maintenance crew, board members, administration, PTO members, etc.
- **Advisory Board:** One student from each homeroom was sent to meetings with the Principal to offer their idea. The students were encouraged to share ideas on how to improve the total environment of the school.
- **Service Learning:** Homerooms chose their service learning projects. One homeroom made buckeye necklaces to raise money for those less fortunate. Several homerooms joined together to donate and walk for "Light the Night." Others provided gifts for Christmas through the Salvation Army's Angel Tree Project. Others visited the local nursing care facilities and caroled and visited the elderly. Many made yellow ribbons and small gifts of candy for our returning servicemen.

Youth leadership team

One high school created a youth leadership team as part of their Asset Building and character initiatives. This group of students, identified by teachers as asset-deficient, received training in the *40 Developmental Assets*. After training, they conducted a professional development workshop for the high school teachers. They planned and led a two hour training filled with hands-on activities, team-building fun, and an opportunity to thank their teachers for the difference they made in the lives of youth.

Character Kids Application

Name:____ Grade:____________

The nine week period that I would prefer to be involved: 1st, 2nd, 3rd, 4th (please circle)
We would like to involve as many students as possible. We would also like to provide choices as to their responsibilities.

Home-base Teacher:____

Study Hall Teacher____

Please rate yourself on the following virtues:
(1 is minimal, 2 is slight, 3 is average, 4 is strong, 5 is outstanding.)

Responsible/Reliable	1	2	3	4	5
Respectful	1	2	3	4	5
Honest	1	2	3	4	5
Caring	1	2	3	4	5
Leadership skills	1	2	3	4	5

Would you be a good role model for other students? Yes No

Why? ____

Please share why you would like to be a Character Kid:

Your grades are a priority. Do you have the extra time that is needed for this responsibility? Yes No

Are you willing to share information and be a leader in your Home-Base? Yes No

Have you had any experience as a leader? If so, please share that experience.

Home-Base Teachers' Signature for Recommendation: ________________________

Academic Teachers' Signature for Recommendation: ________________________

Parent's Signature for Permission:________________________________

This leadership team then shared the assets with a community group comprised of local business people. They challenged them to take the assets into their homes and workplaces. Next, they held an asset retreat for 25 of their at-risk fellow classmates who needed that extra support at this time in their lives. Traveling by bus to a local church, they spent the entire day discovering and building upon their strengths, as well as building relationships with fellow classmates. One of the strongest results was that more than half of the at-risk group stepped up and volunteered to lead the middle school retreat which was planned for the following month.

Renaissance

One school had been using Jostens Renaissance[34] program to develop student leadership and recognize students for "displaying positive attitudes, exemplary behavior, attention to academics and attendance." It is based on the premise that the students who get the most recognition in schools are athletes, top students and those with discipline problems. The program recognizes and celebrates the often overlooked students, those who follow the rules, come to school and work hard. Because the program can be customized to the school and community, this school was able to incorporate their service learning projects, leadership activities and emphasis on good character and citizenship into the program. It was a good fit because all students had the opportunity to participate.

Leadership luncheon

One of the schools began the year with a leadership luncheon for all eighth grade students. In preparation, students completed a reflective survey in their English classes, asking them to evaluate the eighth grade class—what were its strengths, what were the weaknesses, and what were their suggestions to improve the class? They also asked students to bring in a variety of non-perishable foods. On the day of the luncheon, students listened to a speaker talk about character and compassion, and then broke into groups led by high school students to discuss targeted character traits such as citizenship, civility, empathy, etc. Lunch was provided by the PTO, and in the afternoon, students created food baskets for the needy with their canned goods, and discussed the results of the reflective survey about the class strengths and weaknesses. They created an action plan to improve the class. Later in the year, the plan was revisited during another class meeting to see if progress had been made.

This district used a similar format for a leadership luncheon in the high school, focusing on team-building. The speaker talked about *TENspiration*—ten things students can do to change the world. The ten strategies are listed in the box below.

TENspiration!
10 things you can do today to inspire the world around you.

1. Create connections that count.
2. Set aside your own wants and needs to be a part of something bigger.
3. Overcome your fears and obstacles.
4. Create ways to be inclusive of others.
5. Practice unconditional acceptance, demonstrate enthusiastic support, and overcome judgment.
6. Look to be inspired.
7. Inspire with intent, but not expectations.
8. View inspirational moments as their own reward.
9. Know that inspirational moments happen every day.
10. Create your own inspirational moments.

After the speaker talked about *TENspiration*, the students broke into groups to discuss and plan service projects to make their community a better place, using the planning guide below.

TENspiration. Change the world. Do something.
How is the school your community?

With your group, create an action plan to help make your school a true community. What needs to be done? How can we make our high school years meaningful and purposeful? What does it take to make our entire student body and staff see the school as a community?

What do you want to do?

Who and/or what is the target of your plan?

Why should everyone care about your plan? Why is it important?

Who must be onboard to make this happen?

How will your vision be implemented? Create a timeline.

What materials and/or funds are needed?

After leadership events, especially those that take class time, it is important to have students evaluate and reflect on their experiences. The following is an example of a leadership day evaluation and reflection form for students.

LEADERSHIP DAY EVALUATION FORM

Thank you for attending today's event! We are glad you were here. As we move forward with our Leadership Group, we want your input on how things went today and where we are headed in the future. Please take a few minutes to reflect on your experiences and give us your feedback about today's activities.

Please rank the following parts of today's activities on a scale of 1 to 3.
Use the following guidelines:

1: Needed Major Improvement/Not a Productive Activity

2: Average/Somewhat Productive Activity/No Feeling Either Way

3: Excellent/Very Productive/Enjoyable

Activity	**Score** (1, 2, or 3)	**Comments** (Very helpful)
Team Building Activities		
Small Group Discussion 1 "How is the school your community?"		
Small Group Discussion 2 "Creating an Action Plan"		

What was the best part of this event today? Why?

Looking ahead, what ideas or activities would you like to see this group do? (These can be things we do at future Leadership Luncheons or they can be ideas of things we do in our school community.)

Other Comments/Suggestions:

Notes

34. http://www.jostens.com/educators/edu_svcs_lp_renaissance.html

10

Discipline

Many schools decide to implement a character education program when they believe that discipline problems have gotten out of control. A few of our project schools were approaching this situation, and wanted to be pro-active. All benefited from the revised emphasis on character and personal responsibility. We found the following principles most helpful to schools as they sought to revise their discipline procedures to align with the character education goals of the project.

Align discipline code to touchstone and shared values

The factor we stressed most with all project schools was to use the shared values of their touchstone as the "common language" upon which to build their discipline code. Most principals found it useful, when talking to a student who had violated the discipline code, to refer to the touchstone or shared values. They could talk about whether they were being respectful of other students or staff members and their property, or being a caring, responsible school citizen. It was very important that the parents and school worked together to help the students learn proper behavior, and that students knew the consequences for inappropriate behavior.

Sending the discipline code home each year and asking parents to sign, is not an effective strategy to control discipline problems. To align with the goals of our project, we asked schools to be more deliberate and intentional with their discipline procedures. We encouraged schools to have an explicit "contract" between parents, students, and teachers at the beginning of the year. This contract ensured that all participants were on the same page.

Opposite is an example of a middle school's contract. The contract does not take the place of a formal discipline code, but by being simple and requiring both the student and the parent to sign it, it increases the chance that parents are aware of the behavior expected of their student. For the most part, the code of conduct is worded in positive terms, which tells students what *to do*, not what *not to do*. To be used effectively, a contract such as the one below needs to be discussed with and defined for students, with periodic reminders and consistent follow-through. As discussed in Chapter 8, if teachers don't consistently enforce the rules, students will learn they are "on paper" only and not abide by them. Inconsistent enforcement also leads to "You didn't punish so-and-so for doing that, why me?" We discuss consistency and enforcement below in more detail. Contracts with students also provide an excellent *teachable moment* to help students understand what a contract is, and what the responsibilities and penalties are for violating a contract.

Consistency and enforcement

Most schools had a "mish-mash" of discipline rules and infractions that were inconsistently enforced and often based on staff preferences. We stressed that to align to the *Smart & Good* model, behavioral expectations needed to be consistent and designed to produce excellence and ethical behavior. Having consistent policies makes it easier for students—they don't have to remember which teacher permits what! Things such as dress codes, use of cell phones, and hallway behavior need to be consistent and enforced, otherwise students will quickly learn that they can ignore the rules. One middle school had exactly this problem. Even though they had general rules for hallway behavior, none of the staff members were in the hallways to enforce them. This school developed a specific and simple set of hallway rules, posted them and then agreed that staff would be stationed at their doorways to not only greet students but also to monitor hallway rules. They saw dramatic improvement.

Another middle school staff sought to create a unified code based on their shared values and touchstone, but found that there were strong opinions as to what should be expected of students. Eighth grade teachers had higher expectations than did sixth grade teachers. Eventually they agreed to develop a consistent code for each grade level that featured increased responsibility and higher expectations for each grade level. Al-

(school name) Code of Conduct Contract

As a responsible, respectful and caring student, **I will**:

1. Take a signed hall pass with me at all times in the hallway.
2. Be quiet and listen for directions at all times during emergency drills.
3. Be respectful during The Pledge of Allegiance no matter where I am in the building (hallways, stairways, etc.).
4. Complete assignments on time.
5. Utilize Progress Book to make up work due to absenteeism.
6. Demonstrate courtesy and respect towards peers, adults and visitors.
7. Arrive to school and class on time.
8. Come to class prepared with proper materials such as textbook, notebook, work, SSR book, pencil, paper, and other pertinent supplies.
9. Practice behaviors that will not be disruptive to the learning process or the orderly function of the school.
10. Be dressed and groomed in a manner that reflects good taste and will not detract or interfere with the educational environment.
11. Practice integrity in all situations.
12. Respect the property of others and the school.
13. Not leave the building or grounds without permission.
14. Not engage in public displays of affection.
15. Not chew gum.

Disciplinary Actions/Consequences

All teachers at _________________ (school) will follow policy set by the School Board and the school administration. In addition to the (school) behavior plan, teachers and students will develop a set of classroom rules. Once agreed upon, a copy of the rules will be posted in each classroom. Not following school and/or classroom rules may be handled by the individual teacher as follows:

1. Warning
2. Detention—Lunch Time, Before/After School
3. Conference (Office personnel, Grade Level Team, Parent/Teacher and/or Administration)
4. Loss of Privilege or Restrict Privilege
5. Time Out
6. Referral to Individual Assistance Team
7. Office Referral

Student signature ____

Parent signature ____ though there was not 100% agreement, they at least were able to come to consensus as to what would be expected and enforced at each grade level.

The table on page 113 is an example of a behavior plan developed by one school that aligned with their school touchstone and made explicit the expected behaviors in all school settings. However, it is not enough just to hand these out or post them around the school—they will be successful only when they are discussed regularly by all stakeholders with the proper behavior expected and enforced by the entire staff.

Punishment vs. restitution

Punishment for discipline infractions does not help students learn appropriate behavior or lead them to make restitution for property they have damaged or people they have hurt. The goal of restitution is to end student apathy, restore student engagement, and promote responsibility and accountability. We encouraged schools to develop discipline practices that helped students learn why the behavior was wrong (what principle did it violate?), what the consequences were (or could be) and how they could make up for it.

One middle school built their ISS (in-school suspension) curriculum around "other study" (one of the 4 Keys—see page 20). The ISS teacher had students read stories about positive role models (see *Role Models: Examples of Character and Leadership* by Joseph Hoedel[35]) and *The Book of Virtues*[36] and then complete assignments to reflect upon what they read. Students had to write about other ways they could have reacted to the (disciplinary) situation. By helping students think through what they had done, what the consequences had been, and showing them a path to redemption and alternate strategies to cope, they sought to prevent students from getting suspended again. In fact, the ISS teacher commented that he had seen a reduction in students in ISS and joked that he might need to find another job!

TOUCHSTONE-BASED BEHAVIOR PLAN			
	RESPONSIBILITY	**RESPECT**	**PERSONAL BEST**
All Settings	Be on time. Bring required materials. Keep the building clean.	Call all adults by their title and last name. Use Touchstone language.	No excuses. (Failure... never an option!) Do all your work with pride. (Give your best!) Accept the consequences of your actions and words.
Arrival	Go to the restroom. Go to your locker. Go to breakfast or homeroom.	Common areas are "loiter-free." Use an appropriate level of voice.	Prepare for the day. Organize your materials and homework.
Restroom	Flush and then wash your hands. Keep it clean.	Give others privacy.	No hanging out.
Hallway	Use passport. No eating or drinking.	Walk quietly and orderly. Respect personal space. Respectful to the Pledge of Allegiance.	Organize your locker. Help others in need. No hanging out.
Office	Come with a pass. Wait quietly. Return to class promptly.	Wait in front of the counter.	Be polite.
Recess	Return equipment. Stay in assigned area.	Listen to all adults. Include others.	Have fun! Play by the rules.
Auditorium/ Cafeteria	Bring your lunch and coat. Pick up the floor area. Wash table. Stay in one seat.	Talk in an appropriate voice level. Respect personal space.	Use good manners.
Emergency Drills	Listen for directions.	Be quiet.	Think-Safety First! Help others.
Dismissal	Bring your required materials. Keep your locker area clean.	Listen quietly to all announcements.	Exit the building safely.

Notes

35. Hoedel, J. M. (2005). Role Models: Examples of Character and Leadership. Boone, NC: Character Development Group.

36. Bennett, W. J. (ed.) (1993). The Book of virtues, a treasury of great moral stories. New York: Simon & Schuster.

11

Freshman Transition

A primary goal of our project was to improve the transition between middle and high school. We sought to help students develop performance and moral character so that they could make a successful transition to high school, graduate and be successful in postsecondary education, career training, the workplace, and as citizens. Data shows that the largest number of students drop out between the ninth and tenth grade year, due to the failure of students to successfully complete high school coursework, become engaged in the life of the school, or find meaningful and relevant learning experiences.[37] Thus, our first priority was for schools to develop a plan for a better freshman transition.

Most schools had some activities in place for freshman transition, ranging from a visit by eighth graders to the high school to a well-developed and executed "Link Crew" program (see http://www.boomerangproject.com/link/what-link-crew for more info about Link Crew). For some schools therefore, the challenge was to develop completely new transition activities, and for others it was to integrate performance and moral character development into the established programs. While most schools concentrated initially on the aspects of the social transition to high school, as the project progressed they began to pay more attention to the academic issues associated with the transition. For example, one school instituted a "freshman-only" day the first year of implementation to help students adjust, but by the third year of implementation, they began a "Freshman Academy" program to help students who were at risk of failure. For successful transitions to high school, attention must be focused on both the social and academic adjustment.

The remaining sections of this chapter describe the variety of social and academic strategies that were implemented during the course of the project.

"Traditional" freshman orientation

Many schools employ fairly simple transition activities for helping students adjust to the high school (or middle school). Sometimes eighth grade students visit the high school in the spring before they enter high school, some are paired with an upper class "mentor," and sometimes there are events just prior to the start of school when freshmen get their books, schedules and lockers. Sometimes there are social events before high school begins. All of these activities were in place in one form or another in all of our schools prior to the project. They are a good start, but they just scratch the surface of helping students adjust and they don't take into consideration the academic needs of incoming freshmen. Our first challenge to our schools was to make the transition more personal, promote relationship building and incorporate the goals of ethics and excellence.

Transition Survey

One high school surveyed eighth grade students to see what concerns they had so as to better design their transition activities. They asked academic questions, procedural questions and social questions, examples of which are in the box opposite.

Results of the survey were compiled and distributed to staff for use in designing their transition activities and to help staff better understand concerns entering freshmen had about the high school. They also broke down the results by middle school (there were three in the district that fed into the high school) to help staff at each middle school better design their programs and activities for eighth graders.

Transition Survey

Circle the number which is closest to your opinion. 1=Strongly Disagree, 4=Strongly Agree

Academic Questions

1. I am concerned with the increased amount of homework.	1	2	3	4
2. I am concerned about making up work when I am absent.	1	2	3	4
3. I am concerned about staying organized.	1	2	3	4
4. I am concerned about my classes being more difficult.	1	2	3	4
5. I am concerned about an increased responsibility for monitoring my own progress.	1	2	3	4
6. I am concerned about earning good grades.	1	2	3	4
7. I am concerned about taking the "right" classes to prepare for success after high school.	1	2	3	4
8. I am concerned about forgetting things in my locker or at home that I need for class.	1	2	3	4
9. I am concerned about taking tests or exams.	1	2	3	4

Procedural Questions

1. I am concerned about using a new locker.	1	2	3	4
2. I am concerned about finding my way around the high school.	1	2	3	4
3. I am concerned about getting to class on time.	1	2	3	4
4. I am concerned about lunchtime routines.	1	2	3	4
5. I am concerned about learning the rules and procedures at the high school.	1	2	3	4
6. I am concerned about missing the bus.	1	2	3	4
7. I am concerned about the number of passes given by teachers	1	2	3	4
8. I am concerned about discipline procedures.	1	2	3	4
9. I am concerned about strict policies on tardiness and absences.	1	2	3	4
10. I am concerned about not being on teams like the middle school.	1	2	3	4

Social Questions

1. I am concerned about getting involved in clubs.	1	2	3	4
2. I am concerned about making friends.	1	2	3	4
3. I am concerned about getting along with teachers.	1	2	3	4
4. I am concerned about finding someone to eat with at lunch.	1	2	3	4
5. I am concerned about getting involved with sports teams.	1	2	3	4
6. I am concerned about being pressured to try drugs, alcohol, or cigarettes.	1	2	3	4
7. I am concerned about getting into fights.	1	2	3	4
8. I am concerned about belonging to the "right group."	1	2	3	4

"Before school starts" activities

Activity Fair

One school added an activity fair before school started. All school clubs and activity groups had a booth to explain what they did, and also to "recruit" freshmen. A newsletter-type publication was distributed the previous spring to all eighth graders that included a listing and description of all the clubs as well as other transition activities that were planned.

Family Open House

One school found success with a *Family Open House* which was open to freshmen and upper classmen. The freshmen attended separately from the others since they were attending high school for the first time. The gymnasium had a pep rally atmosphere with welcome signs, cheerleaders, and balloons. The sidewalks were chalked with greetings; the high school band played; and all staff greeted students at the door. A treasure hunt was used to help students become acquainted with the school and it produced a fun and inviting activity. They collected stickers from each location (for example the library, nurse's office, gymnasium, etc.) and entered their completed treasure hunt form for a door prize drawing.

Fresh Fest

One high school, that had several middle schools feeding into it, organized a social event for freshmen-only before school started to introduce the students to each other. The event was held at the high school and included prizes, a DJ, dancing, and refreshments.

Freshman-only day

Several of the schools chose to add a freshman-only day at the beginning of school in addition to their traditional high school orientation activities. For the first day of school, only freshmen attended. One school sent formal invitations to each incoming freshman stating that the purpose of the orientation was to make the transition from middle school to high school a positive one. Seniors and juniors served as leaders and mentors to the freshmen. In addition to learning their class schedule and meeting all their teachers the first day without the crowds they would experience the next day, schools planned team-building activities, club fairs, and motivational speakers for this day. One school had collected questions about high school from the students as eighth graders, and they had upper classmen answer these and other questions in small group sessions.

Advisories

One high school added advisories as part of their transition activities. Although all students participated, they developed a separate "curriculum" for freshmen that focused on study skills, time management and relationship building. (See pages 65-66.)

Upper class mentors

Most schools used upper class mentors during their freshman orientation process, but one school decided to maintain those relationships throughout the freshman year. They built time and activities into the year to help students maintain these mentoring relationships. One school went "high tech" with this idea, and created an eighth grade "blog" during the spring semester that was monitored by staff and student mentors for incoming freshmen.

Freshman Academy

After initiating a freshman-only day the first year, one school found that many of the at-risk students needed more support. They formed a "Freshman Academy" designed to provide social and academic support for these students. The principal identified motivated staff members who were invited to participate. Their schedules were modified so that they had common planning time and common lunch periods. These faculty members took responsibility for monitoring the at-risk freshmen and providing them the extra support they needed to prevent failure in their classes. Staff met frequently with each other and the students. They worked with students on skills such as conflict resolution, time management, responsibility and study skills (many of these were performance character skills). They had weekly contact with parents to keep them informed of their student's progress. They also used the program "Top Twenty" (see http://www.top20training.com) to help these students develop the skills and habits that distinguish the "top 20%" of successful students.

"P.R.I.D.E. period"

One school created a freshman specific curriculum that freshmen experienced approximately twice a month during the homeroom period. P.R.I.D.E. stood for **P**ersonal **R**esponsibility **I**n **D**eveloping **E**xcellence. The curriculum was a combination of focused activities and reflective journal writings. The first PRIDE period lesson is in the box below and we have included four other lessons in the appendix (pages 137-142) to illustrate the range of topics. For some of the topics, they also developed a PowerPoint lesson that teachers could use on the topic of the day. From their transition survey, they had identified that many freshmen were concerned about exams, so they developed a PRIDE period lesson on how to prepare for exams that they offered several weeks before the first exams. We have included the PowerPoint slides in the appendix to illustrate how they approached this topic.

PRIDE One

Lesson Title:
PRIDE: What does it mean and why does it matter?

Essential Question:
What does it mean to be a productive member of this High School?

Brief Description of Lesson:
Students will be introduced to the PRIDE period. Students will understand expectations for participation and be introduced to their PRIDE Journal.

Students will brainstorm thoughts and ideas about the meaning of the word PRIDE. This will be done by writing words/phrases on a sticky note and placing them around the word PRIDE, which will be written on the board.

Rationale for Lesson:
It is essential for students to gain an understanding for the hallmark of our school, PRIDE.

Method of Instruction:
Teachers will begin by telling students about the PRIDE period. Teachers will review expectations and discuss the PRIDE journal.

Teachers will then write the word PRIDE on the board and ask students to place their first thoughts on a sticky note. Students will then stick their note onto the board. Once all sticky notes are placed, the teacher will read the responses. A student will be chosen as the recorder.

Journal Assignment:
Now that you know what PRIDE stands for, how will you take responsibility for developing yourself as a student at this High School?

Notes

37. Bridgeland, M., DiIulio, J., & Morison, K. (2006). The Silent Epidemic. Perspectives of High School Dropouts. A report by Civic Enterprises by Peter D. Hart Research Associates for the Bill and Melissa Gates Foundation.

12

Sustainability

School improvement efforts that come about as a result of a grant are difficult to sustain once the grant ends, and most grants provide funding for only a few years—much shorter than the time needed to make real sustainable change. Therefore, when we began the project, we focused on facets that we believed would be sustainable. We believe there are three key factors that help sustain an initiative such as ours:

- Tie initiatives to the school "infrastructure"
- Communicate and celebrate
- Refresh

Tie to the school "infrastructure"

One of the reasons we focused on initiatives such as school touchstones, discipline codes, and classroom procedures is that once established, these become the new "norm" and part of the everyday life of the school. By aligning these infrastructure policies and practices to the goals of ethics and excellence, we sought to make sustainable changes that would persist once the project was over. If you are undertaking a character education program in your school, these are the important features that will help you establish and sustain a program.

Communicate and celebrate

Communication is key to any new initiative. To be successful, students, staff, parents and the community must be made aware of the efforts and impact of the program. Make communication an integral responsibility for a sub-group of your character committee, giving them the job of actively promoting and publicizing what you are doing. Ask for "space" in the school newsletter, or on the school webpage. Ask for a few minutes at staff meetings to keep everyone informed. This does not take a lot of time, but will pay off in maintaining awareness and intentionality by everyone to promote performance and moral character. Maintain the language developed in the touchstone and tie any new initiatives to the character development goals. Show how performance and moral character can add power to other school improvement efforts.

Celebration of success and recognition of students will also keep a program going because recognitions help build positive community. No one wants to sacrifice academic time to what many consider as "fluff," but without the celebrations and positive experiences of activities like a "leadership day," students and staff get burned out. Positive relations and climate will pay dividends in greater focus and accomplishment in classes.

Refresh

All programs become stale eventually. Staff and student turnover often results in a community that doesn't remember why certain programs were started. Community demographics change and academic requirements are altered. Therefore, it is important to periodically revisit any initiative to see if it needs to be revised. One district (not in the project) that had adopted a character education program a decade earlier, found that the values were no longer a good fit for the high school. They revisited the selection of their shared values and created a new touchstone. The revision sparked the imaginations of students and staff and led to the creation of new programs to meet new needs of a growing at-risk population. Even without this kind of change, it is important to revisit items such as discipline codes and grading systems periodically to make sure they still "make sense."

Final thoughts on sustaining your initiative

- It's not all about you; it's about what is working for your school as a whole.
- You can't expect change in students before change takes place in teachers.
- Effective leadership promotes effective change.
- Change that is gradual gains momentum. Patience is key to the success of your initiative. Pushing reluctant staff to participate in something they do not believe in will not immediately result in success. Rather, gather up the ones that are on board and want to be leaders. We have found that other staff will jump on board over time especially when they witness the success in the early adopters' classrooms!

A Summary of the Positive Results Produced by the Ohio Partnerships in Character Education Project: Creating Smart and Good Schools

By Michael W. Corrigan and Doug Grove

In a time when curriculum is basically the sole input for educational improvement and test scores are the dictating output for determining success in today's education world, it is rare to find educators willing to try a non-curriculum based approach to school reform. And when accountability rests mainly on improving achievement and proficiency scores, it is even rarer to find educators who are willing to focus on what some might wrongly believe to be an unproven prosocial education intervention; centered on developing character. As this short summary will show, however, the majority of educators who took part in the *Ohio Partnerships in Character Education Project: Creating Smart and Good Schools* were an exception to the norm. As a result, many of the educators in this grant project implementing the intervention discovered that sometimes in order to make real change, schools must often expand their school improvement efforts beyond a focus on curriculum. The results to be shared in this chapter from the four year research project with Ohio schools, funded by the US Department of Education's Partnerships in Character Education initiative, will show that schools with educators that infused character based educational strategies made greater gains in achievement, school climate and student attitudes than schools that did not.

The Goal and Objectives of the Project

The goal of the Ohio Partnerships in Character Education (CE) project was to design and implement character education models that could be integrated with the state content standards, existing curriculum, and could also be carried out in conjunction with other school improvement efforts. These improvement efforts included the development of student moral and performance character to insure their success in school and beyond. Specifically, the objectives were to improve achievement and high school success for all students (especially underrepresented populations) by establishing CE models that targeted:

- the development of both performance and moral character
- improvement in school climate by designing and implementing professional development and school strategies to assist teachers and school staff in creating classroom environments that are supportive and challenging for all students
- and to increase parental, community and staff involvement by insuring all stakeholders had a voice in developing and implementing policies, strategies, and resources to help schools develop a culture of excellence and ethics for all students

The Basic Approach to the Study

To begin this project, ten Ohio school districts were randomly selected from a pool of 23 applicants to participate in the study that sought to improve student achievement, school climate, parent involvement, and help middle school students make successful transitions to high school. Half of the schools (5) were assigned to an intervention group (expected to put in place character education) and the remaining five served as a comparison group (expected to not focus on character education). The intervention schools received training on the "Smart & Good Schools" model (Lickona & Davidson, 2005) , a research-based school improvement model that uses the development of student moral and performance character to maximize student learning. To review, moral character is defined as those shared values that help students get along with others—compassion, respect, fairness, responsibility, and cooperation. "Performance" character is defined as those qualities that have a mastery orientation—such as perseverance, diligence, work ethic, self-discipline and positive attitude. Intervention schools also had the services of a trained "character coach" whose role was to disseminate the professional development throughout the staff and provide classroom coaching on instructional strategies to develop performance and moral character in the classroom.

Each year, Multi-Dimensional Education Inc. (MDed) led an external evaluation team to collect data from both intervention and comparison schools using the MDed's Multi-Dimensional Assessment to evaluate the attitudes, perceptions and beliefs of students, staff and parents (see www.MDedInc.com for more information on the MDA). Annual survey data was collected following American Psychological Association guidelines either in large group settings (e.g., auditorium or cafeteria) or small group settings such as English classes. This assessment data was collected every year in May on participating educators, parents, and students in both the intervention and comparison schools. Each year the intervention schools received training on the Multi-Dimensional Assessment reports, and how to use the reports to make more informed data-driven decisions. The following table shows the cohorts and data collection timeline:

Table 1: Data Collection Timeline

Cohorts	May 2007 testing: Baseline	May 2008	May 2009	May 2010
Cohort 1	7th grade	8th grade	9th grade	10th grade
Cohort 2	6th grade	7th grade	8th grade	9th grade

The Multi-Dimensional Assessment (MDA)

To better explain how the survey data was collected, the following is a brief description of the dimensions assessed by the MDA; the selection of which was based on more than 40 years of research that found these factors to be meaningful to educational success (Corrigan, Grove & Vincent, 2011). Each dimension is assessed by using an assortment of reliable and validated proprietary scales developed correctly and field tested by the research/evaluation team on close to 35,000 participants within random trials studies. Please note that these scales have been adapted to measure and triangulate the opinions of staff and parents in relation to the students.

Community Engagement

An abundance of research has shown how Community Engagement is quite beneficial to academic success. A sense of community can provide benefits in terms of increased student achievement and motivation to learn (Bryk & Driscoll, 1988; Comer & Haynes, 1991; Welhage, Rutter, Smith, Lesko & Fernandez, 1989). Community Engagement also can reduce student feelings of alienation which interacts with school climate (Bryk, Lee, & Holland, 1993; Welhage et al., 1989). It can create a more engaged community that goes beyond benefiting students and also benefits teacher morale and collegiality, teacher-administrator relationships, and even school-parent-community relationships (Bryk & Driscoll, 1988, Comer & Haynes, 1991).

This dimension assesses factors such as:

- Interpersonal Community Engagement (measures students' level of community communication)
- Parent Involvement (in school and community)
- Service to Community (measures students' level of service to community and their view of the participation of others in the school)

Developmental Perspectives

There is an abundance of foundational theory that many were provided most likely as a pre-service teacher that supports this dimension. You probably remember learning about Locke, a British philosopher who viewed the child as a tabula rasa, or "blank slate." According to Locke, in the beginning of one's life we start with nothing and it is the experiences that we gather that shape us. Erickson's (1950) psychosocial theory of development illustrates that in some stages of development children need to autonomously expand their intrinsic initiative and ask themselves questions related to who they believe they are and what is their place in society. However, at each stage of Erickson's model the child acquires attitudes and skills that contribute to the development of an active, contributing member of society. Therefore, in a number of Erickson's stages a child is somewhat reliant upon the role of and interaction with parents, teachers, adults, and peers to help in the process. Vygotsky, in his sociocultural theory, purported that these social processes are what account for the higher mental processes not always gifted through genetics (as cited in Wertsch, 1985). Psychologists such as Bruner believed "that individual development could not be understood without reference to the social and cultural context within which such development is embedded" (Driscoll, 2000, p. 240).

This dimension assesses factors such as:

- Student Success Traits (measures the level of student understanding of various character traits such as honesty, respect, and trust, and the extent to which students say they practice those traits)
- School Misconduct (measures student report of how often students break school rules, cheat or get in trouble in school.)
- Compassion for Others (measures how much a student thinks and cares about others)
- Good Deeds (measures how often a student has helped others)

Educational Attitudes

GPA and standardized testing supposedly offer insight into one's hypothesized academic achievement. Yet most of us know a smart child who is not motivated to learn or take a test. Motivation is the key to learning, and improving educational attitudes is the answer to increasing motivation. How about considering the students' feelings toward school or testing? How about seeking more information as to how one might build an intrinsic drive to learn? This dimension is focused more specifically on the development of students' attitudes toward education. The field of Educational Psychology is an "academic discipline that studies and applies concepts and theories of psychology to instructional practice" (Ormrod, 2006, p. 4). Basically the field of Educational Psychology studies how learners learn and what variables help them to be successful. There are a great number of variables (e.g., affect—feelings and emotion for a task, motivation, goal setting, self-efficacy) that hold great potential for helping students achieve higher learning. For decades motivation has been studied by a great number of psychologists such as B. F. Skinner. What we have found is that motivation is one of the keys to learning. If a child is not motivated to learn about a subject, the level of intelligence of the student or educator does not matter. If a student does not believe they are empowered to be good at a subject, they will lack the confidence they need to be successful. If they lack motivation, self-efficacy, academic empowerment and positive feelings for school or subject matter this will provide many challenges to the educator.

This dimension assesses factors such as:

- Motivation to Learn (measures how motivated a student is to learn)
- Personal Academic Empowerment (measures how empowered a student feels about school and their academic success)
- Student Work-Ethic (measures how hard a student works on academics)
- Feelings for School (measures how a student feels about school)

Faculty Fidelity

Student-teacher relationships encompass trust, fairness, and student perceptions on how much teachers care about them. The adage "students don't care how much you know until they know how much you care" holds true. How well are teachers teaching? How well are they respected? The fidelity (devotion, loyalty, and faithfulness) of teachers is the true indicator of teaching success. Educators can be "highly qualified" (i.e. have a certification or degree saying they know what they are teaching) but still not have the fidelity to be a successful teacher.

This dimension assesses factors such as:

- Teacher Trust (measures how much students trust teachers, think they treat students fairly and are honest)
- Teacher Satisfaction (measures student perceptions of how teachers feel about their work- are they satisfied, positive and committed?)
- Teacher Belief in Students (measures student perceptions as to how much teachers believe in students, want to and help them to succeed)

Leadership Potential

Principals and leadership teams are critical to the success of creating an organizational culture for instructional and professional success. With poor leadership at the foundation of the organization, success will rarely ever materialize. Assessing organizational management practices and communication is essential for academic achievement. How do the teachers feel about your principals? How do the children feel about the leadership teams?

This dimension assesses factors such as:

- Leadership Satisfaction (measures how satisfied the stakeholders are with school leadership)
- Principal Trust (measures how much students trust principals)
- Leadership Communication (measures the level of communication provided by leadership)
- Leadership Shared Mission and Vision (measures the connectedness of shared mission and vision between stakeholders)

School Climate

Student's positive connectedness and relationships with others in school has been shown to promote student's psychological health, (Kasen, Johnson, & Cohen, 1990; McNeely, Nonnemaker & Blum, 2002; and Whitlock, 2006), help develop a positive self-concept in students (Reynolds, Ramiez, Magrina, & Allen, 1980), reduce bullying within a school (Peterson & Skiba, 2001), and reduce anti-social behavior (Kuperminc, Leadbeater, Emmons, & Blatt, 1997). Safe and caring schools are a necessity for a student/teacher relationship to grow. The emotional attachment of a student to his or her school is critical to a good education, and the school climate is a major impact on this attachment and academic achievement. How do students, parents, and educators feel when they walk through the school doors? Do students, parents, and educators feel safe? Does the school offer a positive learning environment?

This dimension assesses factors such as:

- (MDED) School Climate (measures the school climate and perceived environment)
- Student Relationships (measures the quality of relationships between students)
- School Liking (measure how much students like their school)
- School Isolation (measures to what extent students feel isolated within the school)

Please note that normally, the MDA also assesses an additional dimension focused on Curriculum Expectations. But in order to fit in additional scales related to performance and moral character this dimension was omitted from the study. Regardless, for use in this study's analysis we utilized the scales within each of the MDA's dimension to produce an educational index comprised of 3 to 5 sub-scales as described above. By doing this we were able to create 6 index scores instead of the 20+ scales on the full MDA's protocol. Such an approach in our opinion provides for a more meaningful, robust analysis and findings that educators can more easily conceptualize and apply.

Additional Data Collected

Beyond collecting the Multi-Dimensional Assessment survey data we also collected academic achievement data (e.g., achievement test scores, GPA) and academic challenge data (e.g., behavior incidents, attendance) pertaining to and associated with each participating students' unique ID number. We also collected data on variables to be used for covariates in the deeper analysis such as socio-economic status, ethnicity, and other variables statistically associated with academic achievement. Some of the other variables obtained from district and school records were: percent of students receiving free/reduced school lunch, and student and teacher demographic characteristics. Yet, in order to determine how or what improves academic achievement, one must also assess the process and fidelity of the intervention taking place. Therefore, we also used our Character Education Infusion Rubric (CEIR) to determine quantitatively and qualitatively to what extent the intervention was embraced and implemented. The CEIR was developed for use as a process evaluation assessment tool to be completed by educators. The intent of the CEIR is to assess the level and quality of Character Education being implemented and infused within the participating schools from the perspective of the educators in the building.

The Results

After four years of the project, all data were analyzed and results confirmed that the intervention schools had in fact infused the character-based intervention, and that they produced statistically significant higher achievement scores and GPAs compared to the comparison schools. Over the course of the project, qualitative changes were observed in the way these schools and educators approached their peers, students and parents. The intervention schools adopted a character-based philosophy that challenged many of them to focus more heavily on developing performance and moral character and in the process, changing their own perspectives on education, while simultaneously staying focused on academics. Staff were coached on how to change the way they taught, not what they taught. The survey data assessing student attitudes identified that students in the intervention schools experienced statistically significant improvement in parent involvement, willingness to participate in community service, understanding of character traits, positive attitudes toward teachers, and more positive ratings of the overall school climate. The educators in the intervention schools showed similar increases in perspectives.

To be more specific for those with greater knowledge in analysis and statistics, the results suggest that during the time of the grant project the intervention schools infused a statistically significant higher amount of character education into their efforts. The findings from the posttest process assessment using the CEIR and performing ANOVAs (Analysis of Variance) and t-Tests suggest that statistically significant differences developed over the four years of the grant intervention with intervention schools showing higher posttest levels related to integrating character education on: Implementation; Multi-dimensional character education (CE); CE Curriculum Integration; Student Bonding; CE-based Leadership; Professional Development; Community/Parent Involvement; and CE Specifics.

The Wilk's Lambda test within the MANCOVA (Multivariate Analysis of Covariance) analysis shows that all the effects are highly statistically significant. The results support that the homogeneity of variances assumptions were met for all variables (Reading, Math, Writing and GPA). Analysis supports that, when controlling statistically for baseline measures of achievement, the intervention schools produced higher scores than the control schools in reading, math, writing and GPA.

As for results pertaining to the federally mandated GPRA (Government Performance and Results Act) measures captured by the Multi-Dimensional Assessment survey from the student perspective, the Wilk's Lambda test shows that with the exception of Educational Attitudes and

Leadership Potential, the effect is statistically significant with intervention schools showing statistically significant higher scores on the posttest survey data while statistically controlling for baseline scores. This suggests that the intervention schools (from the participating students' perspective) at the end of the grant had produced higher levels of community engagement, developmental perspectives (character), faculty fidelity, and school climate.

Due to a substantial amount of turnover in staff and faculty, we were not able to perform a MANCOVA on the educators' perceptions. We did not have a sufficient amount of pre and posttest MDA survey data to use. Therefore, Analysis of Variance (ANOVA) was used to determine whether the MDA dimensional scores differed among control and intervention staff respondents. The analysis showed that there are statistically significant differences with intervention schools reporting higher scores for Community Engagement, Educational Attitudes and Leadership Potential dimensions but not for others. However, Developmental Perspectives (measures of character) were nearly significant with $p = .057$.

The analysis suggests that strong evidence exists supporting the conclusion that the intervention schools taking part in the character education study experienced many benefits during the 4 years. The intervention schools showed statistically significantly higher test scores and GPAs compared to the comparison schools. The intervention schools from the students' perspectives improved in community engagement, developmental perspectives (character), faculty fidelity, and school climate. The educators in the intervention schools showed similar increases in perspectives. Project director Dr. Lucy Frontera, Executive Director of Ohio Partners in Character Education, commented on the positive results, "What is most encouraging is that we were just getting started on some of the initiatives and changes we were trying to make. To get positive results with the turnover in personnel we experienced in some schools and a major budget cut in the final year, tells me that we were on the right track. I'm convinced that had we been able to continue longer, the results would have been even stronger!"

References

Bryk, A. S., & Driscoll, M. E. (1988). *The school as a community: Theoretical foundations, contextual influences, and consequences for students and teachers* (Report WP 88-11-05). Chicago: The University of Chicago Benton Center for Research in Curriculum and Instruction.

Bryk, A. S., Lee, V. E., & Holland, P. B. (1993). *Catholic schools and the common good*. Cambridge, MA: Harvard University Press.

Comer, J. P., & Haynes, N. M. (1991). Meeting the needs of black children in public schools: A school reform challenge. In C. V. Willie, A. M. Garibaldi, & W. L. Reed (Eds.), *The education of African-Americans* (pp. 67-71). New York: Auburn House.

Corrigan, M. W., Grove, D., & Vincent, P. F. (2011). *Multi-dimensional education: A common sense approach to data-driven thinking*. Thousand Oaks, CA: Corwin Press.

Driscoll, M. (2000). *Psychology of learning for instruction*. Needham Heights, MA: Allyn & Bacon.

Erickson, E. H. (1950). *Childhood and society*. New York: W. W. Norton.

Kasen, S. N., Johnson, P. N., & Cohen, P. N. (1990). The impact of social emotional climate on student psychopathology. *Journal of Abnormal Child Psychology*, 18(2), 165-177.

Kuperminc, G. P., Leadbeater, B. J., Emmons, C., & Blatt, S. J. (1997). Perceived school climate and difficulties in the social adjustment of middle school students. *Applied Developmental Science*, 1, 76-88.

Lickona, T., & Davidson, M. (2005). *Smart & good high schools: Integrating excellence and ethics for success in school, work and beyond*. Cortland, NY: Center for the 4th & 5th Rs. Washington, DC: Character Education Partnership.

McNeely, C. A., Nonnemaker, J. M., & Blum, R. W. (2002). Promoting school connectedness to school: Evidence from the National Longitudinal Study of Adolescent Health. *Journal of School Health*, 72, 138-146.

Ormrod, J. E. (2006). *Educational psychology: Developing learners* (5th ed.). Upper Saddle River, NJ: Prentice Hall.

Peterson, R. L., & Skiba, R. (2001). Creating school climates that prevent school violence. *The Clearing House*, 74(3), 155-163.

Reynolds, W. M., Ramirez, M. P., Magrina, A., & Allen, J. E. (1980). Initial development and validation of the academic self-concept scale. *Education and Psychological Measurement*, 40(4), 1013-1016.

Skinner, B. F. (1969). *Contingencies of reinforcement*. New York: Appleton-Century Crofts.

Welhage, G. G., Rutter, R. A., Smith, G. A., Lesko, N., & Fernandez, R. R. (1989). *Reducing the risk: Schools as communities of support*. New York: The Falmer Press.

Wertsch, J. V. (1985). *Vygotsky and the social formation of the mind*. Cambridge, MA: Harvard University Press.

Whitlock, J. L. (2006). Youth perceptions of the life in school: Contextual correlates of school connectedness in adolescence. *Applied Developmental Science*, 10(1), 13-29.

APPENDIX TWO, ALGEBRA II LETTER

(Name of School) Department of Mathematics

Dear Students and Parents,

We will be studying Chapters 3-8 in Algebra II this semester. For each chapter section you will be assigned homework in the textbook and/or Practice Workbook. You will be expected to fill out your Notetaking Guide in conjunction with reading each section of the textbook.

Emphasis will be made on your performance in preparing homework and studying in Algebra II. Algebra II is the first class in mathematics that is equivalent to a college course for credit. Each student must realize that completing homework on time is essential to understanding. Homework is important and is the practice that is needed to be ready on test days. Students should try all problems, show all work, and be ready to ask questions. Each lesson builds upon concepts presented in earlier assignments so successful completion of homework will lead to better test scores. Each student should have the following items in class every day: textbook, notebook paper, pencil, pen, and calculator. Falling behind in a semester course makes it extremely difficult to catch up. The student is responsible to ask for the work completed if an absence occurs. The student can call a friend or the parent may call school to receive the assignment if the student must miss school. Students will have resources available to them online for our textbook. We will assume that everyone in the class is a college prep student and will need to have the self-discipline to complete the required work in order to succeed. Each assignment will be collected daily in the "IN" basket or checked during the class and a notation will be placed in Progressbook that the assignment was completed on time. (COT) Homework not completed on time will not be collected. Notetaking Guides will be checked on Chapter Test days and a notation will be made in Progressbook that the Notetaking Guide was COMPLETELY finished BEFORE THE TEST.

Your grade for the six weeks will be based on quizzes, tests, and special projects. Bonus problems are sometimes added to tests but extra credit will not be assigned to make up for missing work or low test scores. Content quizzes will be given at least twice each chapter over material covered in the chapter. Before quizzes are given the students will have practiced the quiz material in class as a part of homework or classwork. Quizzes will be assigned a value of 5 to 50 points.

One retest for each chapter test can be taken if conditions are met for that chapter. Those conditions are:

- Homework assignments for the chapter handed in on time each day.
- Notetaking Guide completed BEFORE the test
- Review assignments (Chapter Practice Test and Review) completed before the test.
- Questions missed on the test reworked correctly and four other examples for each problem missed worked correctly on paper. (A form will be provided to serve as guide for this step.)

(Algebra II letter, page 2)

The date of the retest will be determined on the day after the test. It would be scheduled within five school days of the test, if possible. Chapter tests count as 100 points.

A midterm exam will be given after Chapter Five and a final exam will be given on the next to last day of the semester. Both midterm and final will be worth 200 points. The grading scale for the class is 93%-A, 85%-B, 75%-C, 65%-D.

Every student is encouraged to keep a notebook where ALL papers pertaining to class will be kept. Any mistakes on Progressbook can be challenged with the notebook. Each student will also be expected to keep track of their grades and assignments completed and will be asked periodically to reflect on progress in the class. The student can do this by keeping a listing of completed work or by printing Progressbook reports.

PARENTS: YOU CAN HELP!!!!!! Help your child with a good attitude towards math and stress the importance of homework. Remember you have access to grades 24/7 on Progressbook. Extra help is always available before, during, and after school.

Please do not hesitate to contact me if you have concerns. I can be reached by phone at:____ or by email: _______. I should return your message within 24 hours. I am looking forward to a successful semester.

Sincerely,
Teacher's Name

Return the bottom of this page with your signatures.

Please acknowledge that you have received, read, and understood the information on the Algebra II class.

Student Signature____

Parent or Guardian Signature: ____________________________________

Date ______________________

PRIDE Two

Lesson Title:
Being a LION: What does this mean?

Essential Question:
What does it mean to be a productive member of this High School?

Brief Description of Lesson:
Re-cap of last week.

Students will be placed into small groups to explore two questions:

- What does it mean to be a student here?
- What do we as a school exemplify?

Rationale for Lesson:
It is essential for students to understand that they are now a member of this high school and that they begin to develop a sense of pride for this notion.

Method of Instruction:
Teacher will write the two questions on the board and have the students answer them in small groups. After five minutes of work, students will be asked to share their group's thoughts.

Journal Assignment:
What are you most looking forward to as a member of this high school?

PRIDE Three/Four

Lesson Title:
"To succeed, we must first believe that we can." —Michael Korda

Essential Question:
How can I take ownership of my education?

Brief Description of Lesson:
Students will explore the book "How to Get Good Grades" in order to discover some of the essential components of becoming a successful student.

Rationale for Lesson:
It is essential for students to recognize that they must take ownership of their education and the tools/components in this book will help them to do so effectively.

Method of Instruction:
Teacher will begin by distributing the book "How to Get Good Grades." Students will be instructed to write their names in the book.

Teacher will give a brief overview of the book and explain how this book can help them succeed as a student.

Students will take the inventory "What Kind of Student Are You?" on page one and then use this information to complete page two.

Students will then be broken off into pairs/groups and assigned one of the "Ten Easy Steps" to summarize and present to the class. Students will then present their information during the PRIDE Four period next week.

PRIDE Four: Students will be given three-five minutes to review their material before presenting to the class.

Journal Assignment:

PRIDE Three: Were you happy with the score that you received on your inventory? Why or why not? How do you plan to improve as a student this year?

PRIDE Four: Of all the steps presented in class today, which one do you feel you most need to improve on? How will you do so?

PRIDE Five

Lesson Title:
Student Behavior: Do the Right Thing!

Essential Question:
How does my behavior determine who I can become?

Brief Description of Lesson:
Students will read through scenarios common to high school. Students will work in groups to discuss the correct response.

Rationale for Lesson:
As students are put in a mock situation and asked to consider the correct actions, they will experience, to a limited degree, the decision making process necessary for correct choices.

Method of Instruction:
Teacher will break students into five groups. Each group will be given a scenario to read and discuss. Students will be given ten minutes to complete their discussion. Students will then present their scenario and thoughts to the class.

Journal Assignment:
Does your behavior affect how you are perceived and who you become? Do you like what your behavior says about you?

PRIDE Fourteen

Lesson Title:
Where do I even begin?

Essential Question:
What should a student do in order to prepare for exams?

Brief Description of Lesson:
Freshmen students need to learn the basics and importance of preparing for exams. The attached PowerPoint will present this information and lead to discussion among students and teachers.

Rationale for Lesson:
It is important for students to understand the importance of exams and be given strategies to help with preparation.

Method of Instruction:
Step one: Teacher reviews the exam schedule with students and answers any questions students may have about the schedule

Step two: Teacher presents the PowerPoint. Teacher can present the slides or have students present the different tips and strategies highlighted on each slide.

Step three: Students will complete journal assignment.

Journal Assignment:
What one piece of advice that you heard today do you plan on incorporating into your life as a student? How do you hope it will impact you?

PRIDE PERIOD—1.6

Exams! Where do I even begin?

Exam Schedule

	Wednesday, January 13	Thursday, January 14	Friday, January 15
Exam/ Announcements 7:35-9:17	Period 8 Exam	Period 1 Exam	Period 7 Exam
Examination 9:34-11:09	Period 3 Exam	Period 2 Exam	Period 4 Exam
Examination 11:26-1:01	Period 5 Exam	Period 6 Exam	Make-Up Exams

PRIDE PERIOD—1.6

Preparing for Exams:

Tips and Strategies for studying the right way!

PRIDE PERIOD—1.6

General Items to Keep in Mind:

- Have a set place to study. (Your room, the library, the kitchen table)
- Know what the test is going to cover
- Make a plan. Know exactly what you need to get done
- Take breaks. Set a time limit. Study 30 minutes then take a break and come back to your task after getting a snack or stretching.
- Have a family member or friend quiz you on the information.

PRIDE PERIOD—1.6

Keep in mind that you want to be an *active* learner, not a passive one.

- The more you use and manipulate the information, the better you will understand it.
- Using and manipulating information in as many ways as possible also maximizes your ability to access your memory.

  —Create a mnemonic device.

  —Make the information into a song.

PRIDE PERIOD—1.6

Do not wait until the night before an exam to study!

- Create a plan in advance of how you will study and stick to it.
- Break down the large task of studying into smaller parts.

PRIDE PERIOD—1.6

If your instructor hasn't explained to you how he or she designs exams, *ask*.

This is a perfectly legitimate concern. Ask what topics the exam will cover. Ask if you will receive a study guide.

PRIDE PERIOD—1.6

A good first step in preparation is to **read through your note**s a couple of times. While you are doing this, you might also:

1. **Highlight** major topics and subtopics, with the goal of generating an outline of your notes.
2. With a second color, **highlight** all vocabulary terms

PRIDE PERIOD—1.6

The more ways you can manipulate and experience the material you are trying to learn, the more secure your understanding and memory will be. Some suggestions:

1. Make **charts**, **diagrams** and **graphs**.
2. Make **lists**.
3. If the subject matter includes structures, practice **drawing** those structures. Remember that a drawing is useless unless the important structures are labeled.

PRIDE PERIOD—1.6

There are almost always types of information which you will have to memorize (vocabulary).

No one has ever invented a better device for memorizing than **flash cards**.

PRIDE PERIOD—1.6

Never, ever pull an "All-Nighter" on the night before an exam.

What you may gain from extra study time won't compensate for the loss of alertness and ability to concentrate due to lack of sleep.

PRIDE PERIOD—1.6

On Exam Day:

- Try not to "cram" during every spare moment before an exam. This only increases the feeling of desperation which leads to panic, and then to test anxiety.
- Be physically prepared.
  - a. Get a good night's sleep.
  - b. Eat Breakfast.
  - c. Bring necessary writing materials to the test (at least *two* writing tools, erasers, calculators if appropriate and allowed).
  - d. This may seem silly, but **go to the bathroom** just before the exam. Don't expect your teacher to let you leave to do this during the test!

PRIDE PERIOD—1.6

Journal Assignment

What exam are you most concerned about?
How do you intend to prepare for it?
Write out a plan in your journal.